50 ¢

GROSSET & DUNLAP
Published by the Penguin Group
Penguin Group (USA) Inc., 375 Hudson Street, New York, New York 10014, USA
Penguin Group (Canada), 90 Eglinton Avenue East, Suite 700,
Toronto, Ontario M4P 2Y3, Canada (a division of Pearson Penguin Canada Inc.)
Penguin Books Ltd, 80 Strand, London WC2R 0RL, England
Penguin Ireland, 25 St Stephen's Green, Dublin 2, Ireland (a division of Penguin Books Ltd)
Penguin Group (Australia), 707 Collins Street, Melbourne, Victoria 3008, Australia
(a division of Pearson Australia Group Pty Ltd)
Penguin Books India Pvt Ltd, 11 Community Centre,
Panchsheel Park, New Delhi—110 017, India
Penguin Group (NZ), 67 Apollo Drive, Rosedale, Auckland 0632, New Zealand
(a division of Pearson New Zealand Ltd)
Penguin Books (South Africa), Rosebank Office Park, 181 Jan Smuts Avenue,
Parktown North 2193, South Africa
Penguin China, B7 Jiaming Center, 27 East Third Ring Road North,
Chaoyang District, Beijing 100020, China

Penguin Books Ltd, Registered Offices: 80 Strand, London WC2R 0RL, England

Archie characters were created by John L. Goldwater.
The likenesses of the original Archie characters were created by Bob Montana.

Published by Grosset & Dunlap, a division of Penguin Young Readers Group,
345 Hudson Street, New York, New York 10014. GROSSET & DUNLAP is a trademark
of Penguin Group (USA) Inc. Printed in the U.S.A.

ISBN 978-0-448-45852-6            10 9 8 7 6 5 4 3 2 1

# Chapter 1

"Wow," Kevin Keller said, his blue eyes wide with wonder as he gazed around the partially decorated Riverdale High gymnasium. "This place is really starting to shape up. Leave it to Veronica Lodge to create a gourmet dinner on a cheeseburger budget."

"That's just how I roll," Veronica said without a trace of modesty in her voice. "I either do things first class or I don't do them at all."

On the other side of the gym, Jughead Jones poked his head out from behind the big box of prom decorations he was carrying, his normally sleepy expression suddenly alert.

"Cheeseburgers? Did somebody say there are cheeseburgers?" he asked, hungrily licking his lips, his needle nose twitching in search of the scent of his beloved burgers.

"Calm down, Jughead," Kevin said. "It was just a metaphor."

"Well, if you *met her for* cheeseburgers and didn't include me, my feelings would be hurt!"

Veronica tossed her long dark hair over her shoulder and smiled at Jughead.

"Has anyone ever told you how funny you are, Juggy?" she asked.

"A few people have mentioned it, yeah," Jughead said.

"Well, they were just being kind," she said sweetly.

Jughead dropped the box he was carrying and stuck his tongue out at her. "How would you know? You think being kind just means not whipping the servants."

"All right, let's break it up," Kevin said through his laughter. "Don't make me use my power as chairperson of the prom decorating committee to make things tough for you guys."

Jughead grinned and saluted Kevin.

"Aye, aye, Mr. Chairperson," he said. "But just for the record, *she* started it with all the talk about cheeseburgers."

"Actually, that was me," Kevin said. "And I'll tell you what . . . if we get the rest of these decorations up this afternoon, we'll celebrate with burgers at Pop Tate's. *My* treat!"

"Okay, now you're talking my language," Jughead said with a whoop of delight. He quickly gathered up an armload of colorful crepe-paper bunting and raced off to hang it in place around the gym.

"You sure know how to motivate the troops," Veronica said, laughing. "I don't think I've ever seen Jughead move that quickly."

"Well, I may be the new kid at Riverdale High, but I want this to be the best prom this school's ever seen," Kevin said. "No kidding, Ronnie, thanks for all your help. I couldn't have done it without you."

"Sure you could. It just wouldn't have been perfect."

"You're probably right, although it still would have to be better than my middle school prom. Man, talk about a disaster . . . !" the tall blond boy said.

"I assume you're not just talking about bad decorations?"

"If only." Kevin shook his head.

"Don't tell me a cute guy like you couldn't get a date?" she said in surprise.

"Oh, I had a date . . . just not exactly the date I wanted. Although I don't think I really knew who I was yet back then, you know? And I also wasn't what *anybody* except my mother would call 'cute.' And *she* probably would say I was cute only because she's my mom and she had to. Back in those days, I was more like king of the nerd boys."

"Oh, come on, Kevin," Veronica said. "It couldn't have been *that* bad."

"It was worse! This was before my dad retired from the army, and he had just been transferred again, which meant yet another start as the new kid at school for me. And believe me, the kids there weren't anywhere near as nice as you guys in Riverdale," Kevin said with a grimace. "In fact, some of them were pretty darned nasty . . ."

● ● ●

"Hey, Keller," Elliot Kingman shouted across the lunchroom of Medford Middle School. "With all that metal in your mouth, do you get radio signals? We wanna listen to some music over here."

The other kids at Elliot's table exploded in a chorus of laughter and hooting that rolled across the crowded room to hit Kevin Keller like a runaway train. He hunched his shoulders and tried pretending not to notice. He focused on the plate of franks and beans on the tray in front of him, poking at it with his fork, but his stomach was churning too much to even think of taking another bite. His face burned red hot with humiliation.

Next to him, his friend Samantha Warren said, "Don't listen to that jerk, Kevin. So what if you wear braces? So do half the kids in our grade."

"I know, Sammie," he said miserably. "But they're not also fat with a face full of zits."

"C'mon, Keller," Nicky DeMarco said, "so what if Elliot's handsome, popular, and captain of the lacrosse and soccer teams? You've got something he doesn't have!"

"A comic-book collection?" Kevin said sadly.

"Well, that, too," Nicky said. "But I was talking about an IQ higher than your shoe size."

Kevin risked a glance over at Elliot and his pals. They were the school's clique of handsome guys and pretty girls, the jocks and the cheerleaders, all with perfect teeth and clear skin. They were always together, always laughing and having fun. None of them were ever embarrassed because they were awkward or clumsy. Not one of them had to live in dread about appearing in a bathing suit in swim class or being laughed at when they asked someone out on a date.

So what if they didn't get the highest grades? Nobody made fun of the popular kids for not being at the top of their classes. Kevin had learned several schools back that the rules were different for the cool kids.

Kevin and his friends called themselves the Geek Squad, a name they wouldn't dare to share with anyone else at Medford. There was Sammie, a pudgy, round-faced girl with kinky hair. An aspiring artist, she dressed in baggy black clothes and usually had smudges of paint, ink, or drawing charcoal on her hands and face.

Nicky DeMarco was a short, skinny boy who could figure out and fix any piece of electronic equipment put in front of him. He wore ill-fitting hand-me-down clothes from his older brothers and thick black-framed glasses held together by duct tape, which were always sliding down his nose.

Rounding out their group was Leon Emerson,

as fat as Nicky was thin, and, if possible, with skin even worse than Kevin's. But Leon was smart and funny, once telling Kevin that his dream was to be a stand-up comedian.

Besides being regular victims of the popular kids' taunts, they all shared common interests in comic books, science fiction, multiplayer online video games, and other nerdy pursuits. Sammie, Nicky, and Leon were all good friends and Kevin knew he was lucky to have them.

But still . . .

He couldn't help wonder what it would be like to be one of the popular kids. Not that he wanted to pick on anybody else like they did . . . but it sure would be nice not to be the one who *got* picked on all the time.

With a deep sigh, Kevin pushed away his lunch tray and stood up. "Is everybody done? I've had enough of lunch period for today."

"You're not gonna finish that?" Leon asked, reaching for Kevin's leftover buttered roll.

Kevin shook his head. Leon grabbed the roll and shoved it whole into his mouth. He chewed happily while they gathered up their trays to bring to the trash.

"Hey, you guys headed out so soon?"

Kevin looked over his shoulder to see Timmy Baker walking toward their table with his lunch tray.

Suddenly, Kevin's feeling of gloom lifted. Timmy was something of an oddity at Medford . . . a popular kid who apparently had no problem being seen with the Geek Squad. Tall for his age, with dark hair and smiling eyes, Timmy was not only captain of the swim team and a straight-A student, but a comic-book collector like them. Kevin thought he was about the coolest kid in town. Possibly the entire state.

"Hi, Timmy," Kevin said, quickly sitting back down. "Naw, we weren't going anyplace special. What's up?"

Timmy shrugged out of his backpack and began rooting around inside it.

"I just wanted to give you back that *Steel Sterling* miniseries you loaned me last week," Timmy said. He found what he was looking for, extracting six comic books, each in its own protective Mylar bag with backer board, and handing them to Kevin.

"So, what did you think?" Kevin asked eagerly.

Timmy grinned and reached for one of the

slices of pizza on his tray. "It was every bit as awesome as you said, dude. I don't think I ever read anything by that writer before . . . what's his name again?"

"Harry Shorten. This was the first thing he ever wrote for MLJ, if you can believe it."

Leon swallowed the last of the roll and added, "His first issue of the *Hangman* comes out this week."

"Yeah? I'm definitely going to want to pick that up," Timmy said.

"We're all going to the comic shop after school tomorrow. It's Wednesday, new comic day," Kevin said. "You want to come with us?"

"Yeah, sure. I also want to see if they've got back issues of that *Steel Sterling* mini," Timmy replied.

"Cool," Kevin said. "And after we check out the new comics, we can—"

Suddenly, a loud crash and clatter from the other side of the lunchroom brought all conversation to a halt.

It came, Kevin wasn't surprised to see, from Elliot's table.

The big man on campus was standing, a wicked smile on his face and his fists clenched at his sides. He was looking down at the floor.

Unfortunately, there was no surprise there, either, for sprawled at Elliot's feet was Luke McPhee, surrounded by his spilled lunch.

"Dude, you got beans on my sneaks," Elliot was saying, loud enough for all to hear.

Kevin didn't need to see what had happened to figure it out. Luke, a sullen, quiet boy with unkempt brown hair and dark, sad eyes that never seemed to look directly at anyone, was Elliot Kingman's number one target. The bigger boy had probably tripped Luke on purpose as he passed by the table.

"They're brand-new, McWeenie." Elliot sneered. "What're you gonna do about it?"

With no change in his expression or even a glance up at Elliot, Luke pushed himself to his knees and slowly began picking up his lunch.

"You hear me, man?" Elliot said.

Kevin swallowed hard. His heart pounded in his chest and he felt his face burning in embarrassment for Luke and anger at Elliot. The popular jock had only made fun of Kevin, but he didn't seem to have any problem taking his tormenting of Luke to the next level.

Using a paper plate as a scoop, Luke was

shoveling the spilled franks and beans onto his tray. His calm, deliberate manner seemed to make Elliot even angrier.

"I'm *talking* to you, freak," Elliot shouted. He bent down and grabbed Luke's arm, causing the paper plate to fly from the boy's hand and send beans splattering onto his jeans.

"Oh, dude, now you're just asking for it!"

"C'mon, Elliot," Timmy called out, rising to his feet. "Leave the kid alone, will ya."

Elliot spun around, his cruel little eyes blazing. He looked ready for a fight, but only until he saw who had spoken. Just as quickly as his anger had flared up, it disappeared. He let loose his grip on Luke's arm and took a step back, a big grin spreading across his face.

"It's all good, Timmy," Elliot said with a harsh laugh. "He knows I was just joking around with him. Right, Luke?"

Luke didn't answer. He went back to cleaning the spilled franks and beans off the floor.

Timmy sat back down, picked up his pizza, and took a big bite.

And *that*, Kevin thought, gazing at the dark-haired boy in awe, is why Timmy Baker is the coolest kid in town. No, make that *the world*!

# Chapter 2

Comics Universe was tucked away in a corner of the Medford Mall near the food court. It was a Wednesday afternoon tradition for the Geek Squad to hit the comic shop and then check out and share their new purchases over a snack at the Dunk-A-Muffin.

That Wednesday, Timmy came strolling into Comics Universe a few minutes after Kevin and the others had arrived. He carried several rolled-up posters under his arm and, after greeting his friends, went over to the counter where the owner sat watch over his comic-book empire.

"Hi, Mr. Salerno," Timmy said. "I was wondering if you'd mind putting up a poster for the middle school prom? Ticket sales have been kind of slow, so we thought it would be a good idea to remind kids about it with posters in all the places they hang out."

"Ooh, right," Sammie said as she and Kevin

browsed the display of new comics together. "I forgot the prom's coming up."

"You going?" Kevin asked as he reached for a copy of *Tigerman*, taking it from the middle of the stack.

Sammie shrugged. "I haven't made up my mind yet. You?"

Kevin, inspecting the comic book for any damage that would affect its collectability and value, also shrugged.

"Dunno," he said. "I haven't really thought about it."

"Hey, guys," Timmy said, joining them at the racks.

Kevin looked up from his inspection and smiled at the new arrival. "Hey, is Mr. Salerno going to put up your poster?"

"Yep, right in the front window," Timmy said. "It's going to be a great prom."

"Oh, I grabbed a mint copy of that issue of *Hangman* for you," Kevin said. "It's almost sold out so I wanted to make sure you got one."

"Cool," Timmy said, slapping the other boy on the shoulder. "Thanks, Kev. You're a real pal."

Kevin grinned. "No problem."

"Anyway," Sammie said, "who are you going to the prom with, Timmy?"

"I asked Gail Rollins," Timmy said as he flipped through the comic book. "We've been kind of going steady the last few weeks, I guess. You guys are going, aren't you?"

Sammie looked at Kevin, who said, "Uh, sure. Yeah. I guess so. You wanna?"

Sammie's round face blossomed into a wide smile. "Sure, Kevin. I'd love to."

"Okay. I guess we'll see you and Gail there," Kevin said happily to Tim.

"Great. Make sure you buy tickets," Timmy reminded them. "Now, where are the back-issue bins? I want to find that *Steel Sterling* miniseries."

● ● ●

With new comics in hand, they wandered over to Dunk-A-Muffin.

"I can't stay too long," Timmy said. "I've still got a bunch of places to hit up about these posters."

"I can take some of them and help you," Kevin offered as he bit into his first chocolate-frosted donut. "It'll take less time with two of us doing it so you can hang out a little longer."

Timmy nodded in approval and held up his hand for a high five. "That'd be awesome, man. Thanks."

"No problem," Kevin said, slapping palms and grinning in delight at the other boy's approval.

"You guys get the new *Hangman*?" Nicky asked.

"I got two copies," Leon said, licking the cream oozing from his chocolate custard donut off his fingers. "One to read and one to bag."

"You are *such* a geek." Sammie giggled.

Leon looked down at his T-shirt, emblazoned with the heroes of the Mighty Crusaders across his wide frame and barked out a laugh. "What was your first clue, genius?" He reached into his bag and pulled a comic book from it with sticky fingers. "Anyway, laugh all you want, but I'm the only one of us with one to read *while* I'm eating."

"Not the only one," Sammie said. She sipped her unsweetened ice tea with lemon and took out the latest issue of *That Wilkin Boy*. "I'm just not having a donut, that's all."

"Huh? No sugar-glazed lemon-filled?" Nicky

asked in surprise. "I've never seen you pass up one of those."

Sammie looked coyly at Kevin and then smiled at the other boy. "Well, now that I've been asked to go to the prom, I thought I might skip a few donuts . . . since I've got to get a new dress and everything."

"*You?*" Leon sputtered in shock. "Got asked to the *what?*"

"Have you ever even owned a dress before?" Nicky asked.

"To the prom," Sammie said haughtily. "Don't act so surprised. And, *yes*, I've worn a dress before . . . when I was little. I think."

Nicky pushed his glasses up his nose and blinked in confusion.

"Wait. When did this happen? We've been together at the comic shop all afternoon."

"Tell them, Kevin," Sammie said, poking him in the ribs with her elbow.

"What? It's no big deal," Kevin said defensively.

"*Kevin?*" Leon and Nicky exclaimed at the same time, looking at each other with wide, startled eyes.

"You're going to the prom with Keller? Is

that even legal?" Leon said.

"So, we're both going to the prom at, you know, the same time. And together. That doesn't make it a *date*," Kevin said, blushing.

"I believe that actually is the definition of a date," Nicky said with a thoughtful nod.

"Cut them some slack, guys," Timmy said. "You should get dates yourself and go."

"Us?" Leon said.

"Dates?" Nicky giggled.

"In what universe, dude?" Leon said with a snort.

●●●

"Okay, where am I going to put this last poster?" Kevin muttered to himself.

After they were done with their snack at Dunk-A-Muffin, everyone had gone their separate ways. Nicky and Leon were going to hang out at Leon's house and Sammie announced she was off to do some shopping.

Kevin and Timmy decided to work different sides of the mall so they wouldn't both be bothering the same merchants with requests to put up posters. So far, Kevin had been successful getting them into the video-game store, three clothing shops popular with his classmates, and both the costume jewelry and the sunglasses stores.

Now, with only one poster left, he was running out of ideas, and he really needed to get home and do his homework.

He rode down the escalator to make one last round of his side of the mall.

"Hey, Kev!"

Kevin turned to see Sammie coming out of the T-Shirt Factory with one of their bags in her hand.

"Hi, Sammie," he said. "Don't tell me you're still shopping?"

"All done now. I'm just waiting for my mom to pick me up. How's the poster hanging going?" she asked with a smile.

He held up his remaining poster. "I've got one more to go. Any bright ideas where I can put it?"

"Mmm," she said. "How about the community bulletin board by the front entrance?"

"Well . . . duh!" Kevin said, whacking himself across the head with the rolled-up poster. "I never even thought of that."

"Good thing you ran into me then," Sammie

said. "Let's go. That's where I'm meeting my mom. Do you need a lift home?"

"Sure, thanks."

"It's the least I can do for my prom date," she said.

Kevin chuckled, "Yeah, right. Hey, look . . . there's Timmy!"

Sammie looked where he was pointing and saw their friend. Timmy was perched on the ledge of the large decorative fountain that sat in the center of the mall. It was a popular gathering spot for people to meet and for groups of kids to hang out.

Timmy was with some of his friends from the swim team and several girls from the cheerleading squad, including his current steady Gail Rollins. The tall, slim girl with long, straight, chestnut hair and bright blue eyes was holding his hand and laughing along with the others at something he had just said.

At that moment, Timmy happened to turn and catch Kevin's eye. Kevin smiled and started to wave. But Timmy gave him only a small nod in greeting and then turned his back on him to continue talking to the kids he was with.

"Oh," Kevin said with a grin and a shrug

to Sammie. "I guess he's busy with swim team business, huh? Anyway, we've got to hang this poster and meet your mother, right?"

Sammie stared curiously for several seconds at Timmy, slowly nodding her head. "Uh, yeah," she said at last, turning back to him with a smile. "Right. You know how my mom gets when I keep her waiting. Let's go."

And as they walked away, Sammie threw a quick glance at Timmy.

She saw the other boy was again looking their way, watching them leave with what looked to her like an expression of relief.

# Chapter 3

With only moments to go before the dismissal bell that would end the school week, Kevin felt like a runner at the starting line. His backpack was ready to swing onto his shoulder, his feet were planted firmly on the floor, and he was sitting at the edge of his seat. At the first sound of the bell, he would push off and race out of Medford Middle School and hopefully forget the mostly miserable week he had just experienced.

Not that there hadn't been a few high points, including receiving a B+ on a history paper he thought he had thoroughly botched and getting to hang out with Timmy a few times, but other than that, it had been a week dominated mostly by Elliot Kingman and his buddies.

Since his first day at Medford, Elliot had been on Kevin's case. Bullies had a sort of radar when it came to picking their victims. They could tell at a glance who was fair game.

Kevin could remember the exact moment on his first day when Elliot had spotted him and picked out the new, chubby kid with braces as his prey. Scarcely a day had gone by since that the bigger, more popular boy didn't remind Kevin of his lowly status on the Medford totem pole.

But this week it felt as though Elliot had decided to amp up his verbal attacks on Kevin and make his every waking hour a lesson in humiliation.

He made fun of the way Kevin looked and the way he dressed. He had a hundred stupid jokes about his braces and a hundred more about his complexion. He even made fun of the way Kevin walked and, with the prom fast approaching, had sarcastically asked if Kevin would be bringing his "boyfriend" to the dance.

While some of the kids laughed at Elliot's jokes and a few seemed sympathetic to Kevin's discomfort, most just pretended to ignore the soccer team captain's cruelty, probably relieved that Kevin was the victim and not them.

Kevin also tried his best to ignore Elliot, but he knew he wasn't fooling anybody. He couldn't prevent his shoulders from hunching as though he was trying to disappear inside himself or his face from turning red with embarrassment and anger. It took every ounce of willpower to keep the stinging in his eyes from turning into tears.

And the worst part was, he couldn't help hating himself just a little for not being able to stand up to this bully.

Kevin was snapped out of his dark thoughts by the sound of the bell.

With a sigh of relief, he leaped from his seat and raced to the door. The weekend had just officially started, giving him two entire days where he didn't have to think about Elliot Kingman and his band of bullies.

● ● ●

Kevin decided to take the shortcut home, leaving by the side entrance and cutting across the ball field behind the school. The plan was for Nicky and Leon to come over to his house later that afternoon for a session of Cromus the Barbarian III, a new MMORPG he had recently signed up for, and Kevin needed time to get his chores done before they arrived.

But just as he was about to round the corner of the building, he was brought up short by a chorus of loud and very familiar laughter.

Elliot and his friends!

Well, so much for taking a shortcut, Kevin thought as he turned to go back the way he had come. It was worth the longer walk to avoid a last round of taunts before the weekend.

"Hey, Elliot," one of the voices yelled to be heard above the laughter. "Let's see how fast he can crawl."

"Yeah, dude," another kid hooted. The others all shouted and laughed their agreement.

Kevin's first thought was to wonder who they were picking on now. His second, as he reached for the door was, well, at least it's not me this time!

And his next was to feel ashamed of himself.

That was exactly what he hated about the other kids when *he* was the victim. No one ever stood up to bullies.

Except Timmy!

Timmy had told Elliot right there in the lunchroom to leave Luke alone, and Elliot had backed down. If his friend could do it, Kevin thought, why couldn't he?

Except Kevin knew why. Timmy Baker was big, strong, popular, and not afraid of anything, while Kevin was none of those things . . . and afraid of everything. He was scared of being humiliated. He was frightened of getting beat up. He was even afraid of something he couldn't name, some deep-down truth about himself that he dreaded revealing to his classmates and *to himself*.

"You want your notebook back, *McWeenie*?" Elliot was saying in his loud, taunting tone. "Then come and get it . . . on your hands and knees!"

McWeenie . . . Elliot's nickname for Luke McPhee!

Kevin was frozen in place, his hand on the door handle and his heart thumping in his chest.

"What're you waiting for, McWeenie? Do I gotta teach you how to crawl?"

He wanted to help Luke, he really did, but no matter how hard he tried, he couldn't force his legs to march in that direction. He was too scared. Besides, how was getting beat up along with Luke going to help either of them?

The door started to swing open against his hand. Kevin jumped back. With a small cry of relief, he saw that it was his math teacher,

Mr. Teitelbaum, his briefcase in hand.

The teacher started to smile at his student but saw the stricken look on Kevin's face at the same moment he heard Elliot's mocking tone from around the corner, "Last chance, little Luke!"

"What's going on out here, Kevin?" Mr. Teitelbaum asked loudly.

Kevin looked in the direction of Elliot's voice but said nothing. Mr. Teitelbaum frowned and followed his gaze. One of the kids in Elliot's posse peeked around the corner, then quickly pulled back. By the time the teacher started toward them, Kevin could hear their hurried, whispered warnings and the shuffling of feet on the other side of the building as they ran off.

"Luke?" Mr. Teitelbaum said as he turned the corner. "Is everything all right . . . ?"

Kevin didn't wait to hear the answer. With tears of shame stinging his eyes, he yanked open the door and ran.

# Chapter 4

Colonel Keller was pushing the lawn mower across the small front yard of the cozy little house they were renting on Tree Lane when Kevin got home. His dad, a tall, rugged man who wore his dark brown hair in a neat army regulation crew cut, was dressed in khaki slacks and a white T-shirt with his ever-present dog tags tucked beneath it on a chain around his neck.

Kevin once asked him why he still used a manual mower while all the other fathers had ones powered by gasoline or electricity.

"I don't need to follow around a noisy machine doing all the work when I can be outside enjoying the peace and quiet and getting some fresh air and exercise," David Keller explained with a smile.

Of course, his father actually liked exercise, starting each day with calisthenics and a jog, even on weekends.

Kevin sadly shook his head as he trudged up the street. As much as he loved and admired his dad, he was nothing like him. And probably never would be. He doubted his father—like Timmy—was afraid of anything, especially a bully like Elliot Kingman. Heck, Colonel Keller had been in combat and parachuted from airplanes in the dark of night, facing things Kevin was sure would send him running away, screaming in fear. He knew for a fact that one of the medals his dad wore pinned to his dress uniform had been awarded to him for running *into* enemy gunfire to rescue a wounded man.

But Kevin couldn't even bring himself to confront one kid to help out another.

He waited until his father's back was turned to hurry up the driveway, so he wouldn't have to face him. He was sure all his war-hero dad would need was one glance to be able to tell that his son was a big, fat coward.

"Hey, Kev! How was school today, buddy?"

Colonel Keller had swung around and was pushing the bright red mower toward him, a welcoming smile on his face.

"Hi, Dad," Kevin said. "It was fine. I mean,

it's Friday, so that automatically makes it an okay school day."

"I hear that," the colonel chuckled. He came to the end of the row he was mowing and stopped. "I don't report in again until Monday myself. Hey, we ought to do something over the weekend. It's been a while since you and me just hung out together."

"Sure," Kevin said with a forced smile. "Whatever you want. That'll be cool."

And then, just as he expected, his father was giving him "the look," the one that said he knew Kevin wasn't telling him something.

"Is everything all right, kiddo?"

Kevin shrugged. "Yeah, Dad. Everything's great."

"Really? Because you don't look like someone who's doing great."

"I . . . I guess I'm just a little tired, that's all," Kevin said, sounding like the lamest liar alive, even to himself. "Anyway, the guys are coming over soon and I sort of wanted to get my chores done before they do, so . . . ?"

Colonel Keller was still giving him "the look," but he nodded anyway and said, "Hmm. I need to finish the mowing, but we'll talk later, okay?"

"Yes, sir," Kevin said.

And maybe by then, he thought as he trudged into the house, he would have thought up something to tell his father that he might actually believe.

● ● ●

"Rise and shine, soldier!"

Kevin groaned and pulled a pillow over his head as his dark and quiet bedroom suddenly filled with light and noise.

"Da-aaad!" he mumbled. "It's Saturday, lemme sleep, will ya!"

In response, Colonel Keller opened the window shade.

"I did let you sleep, Kev. It's after ten o'clock. Time to get out of that rack and hit the floor!" his father said in a booming voice, like an army drill sergeant.

Kevin rolled over and tried to burrow deeper under the pillow.

"Just another five minutes," Kevin pleaded.

"Negative, kiddo. We're burning daylight," the colonel said as he yanked the protective pillow and blanket off Kevin.

Kevin risked opening one eye just enough to

see the colonel standing over his bed, dressed in his running clothes, one hand behind his back.

"I hate it when you get all G.I. Joe on me," Kevin said.

"Remember I said we should do something together this weekend, and you said we could do whatever I wanted?" Colonel Keller said with a big grin and a wink. "Well, I want to go for a run with you."

Now both of Kevin's eyes popped open.

"You mean, a run, as in . . . *running*?" he said in disbelief.

"Good guess, Einstein," his dad said, chuckling. He brought his hand out from behind his back and waved a pair of running shorts and an old T-shirt emblazoned with an image of the Shield in front of Kevin before dropping both on his son's head.

"But *I* don't run," Kevin moaned from under the clothing.

"You do now," his father said.

● ● ●

Half an hour later, Kevin was sprawled on his back on the freshly mowed grass in front of his house, sweat pouring from every part of his body that was able to sweat, gasping for breath, and wishing someone would come along and put him out of his misery.

Colonel Keller was standing over him, looking as if all he had done was take a leisurely stroll up and down the driveway even though he had just run the same distance as his son.

"Not bad for your first time, Kev," he said. "You did almost two miles without stopping."

"Or . . . or breathing," Kevin gasped, too tired to lift his head.

"Don't worry, it gets easier the more you do it," his father said, laughing.

"You mean . . . I have to do this *again*?"

"Sure. You need to run every day if you expect it to do you any good."

"If feeling like this is good for me, I'd hate to feel what something that's bad for me is like," Kevin groaned.

Colonel Keller sat down on the lawn next to Kevin and patted his son on the arm. "Anything worth doing takes effort," he said, but Kevin could tell there was something else on his father's mind. He didn't have to wait long to find out what it was.

"How are things going for you here in Medford, kiddo?" he asked.

"Okay, I guess," Kevin said. "The school's pretty good, and I've made a few friends I really like."

"Good," Colonel Keller said with a thoughtful nod. "I know all the moving around we've done because of my job hasn't been very easy for you. I mean, it seems like just as you start to settle into a school and make friends, I get reassigned and we have to take off for somewhere new."

Kevin sat up in alarm.

"We're not moving again *already*, are we?" he asked miserably.

"Oh no," the colonel said quickly. "I'm sorry, Kevin, that's not what I'm getting at. No, I expect we'll be staying put at least through the end of the school year."

"Whew! You scared me for a second," Kevin said in relief.

"The thing is, you're always the new kid in school, and I know how tough that can be," his father continued. "So if you're having any kind of trouble, you know . . . adapting or anything, I hope you'll be able to talk to me about it."

"Sure, Dad," Kevin said with a nod. But he

almost couldn't meet his father's eyes. In fact, he felt like he was sort of lying by not telling him the truth about Elliot's bullying. Worse, he would bet all of next month's allowance that his dad knew he was holding something back from him.

But what was he supposed to do? If he told, Colonel Keller would have to *do* something about it, like talk to Elliot's parents or somebody at school. Then Kevin would be tagged a crybaby and a tattler, which would make even the kids who now just ignored his existence, hate him.

The colonel nodded and said, "Okay, buddy. I just wanted you to know that I'm here for you if you ever want to talk." Kevin could practically feel the disappointment in his father's sad smile.

"I know, Dad," Kevin said. "And, Dad? Just so you know, maybe I'm not crazy about all the times we've had to move, but I really do understand. I mean, what you do is important and I'm proud of you."

"Thanks, Kev, I appreciate that," Colonel Keller said. He reached over and tousled his son's blond hair.

"Come on, you've always been my hero, Dad, you know that."

"You mean I rate as high as the Shield?" his father asked in mock surprise.

"At least!" Kevin said with a grin.

"Hey, speaking of the Shield, I want to show you something. Stand up," Colonel Keller said, getting to his feet.

Kevin did as he was told. He didn't know what his father was up to, but he had a mischievous twinkle in his eyes as he held out his hand and said, "Shake!"

The boy took his father's hand and, suddenly, he found himself flipping through the air and landing on the lawn on his back. He grunted as the wind was knocked out of him, but he was otherwise unharmed.

"What was *that* for?" Kevin stammered, blinking up at his amused father in surprise.

"It's judo, like the Shield uses," the colonel said. "I thought you might want to learn a few martial-arts moves. It never hurts to be able to take care of yourself, you know."

"Thanks, Dad, that sounds cool . . . but next time, give me a little warning, would you?"

Colonel Keller held out his hand to help Kevin to his feet.

"If there's one thing I've learned as a soldier, kiddo, it's that life never gives any warnings," he said. "You've either got to be ready or you'd better just start running."

"You've already got me doing that," Kevin said, smiling and rubbing his backside where he had landed.

"True, but no matter how fast you might be, you're never fast enough to outrun your troubles. It's better to be the kind of man who does the right thing and faces his problems head on," Colonel Keller said. "So, you up for your first judo lesson?"

Kevin realized all at once that they weren't just goofing around anymore. His father *did* know and was helping him the best way he could . . . without forcing him to rat anybody out in the process.

"Yes, sir!" Kevin said.

# Chapter 5

"Two days is way too short a time for the weekend," Leon grumbled as he and Kevin walked to school bright and early the following Monday morning.

"I know what you mean," Kevin agreed. "By the time I do my homework, get a few extra hours of sleep, and clean my room, the weekend is over and I've got to get ready for another Monday."

"We should start a campaign to add a couple of extra days to the week so we get a longer weekend," Leon said. "We could call one of them Extraday and the other one Wendy."

"Wendy is a girl's name," Kevin said, laughing.

"It doesn't have to be," Leon said. "You can name a pet Wendy, so why not a new day of the week?"

"Yeah, but wouldn't it be confusing for people and pets named Wendy?"

"So, let 'em change their names to Sunday!" Leon said.

Kevin glanced at his grinning friend. "This doesn't have anything to do with Wendy Butler, does it?"

"You mean the Wendy Butler who sits next to me in algebra?" Leon asked.

"Uh-huh, that one," Kevin said with a nod.

Leon shrugged, but when he looked over at Kevin, he was smiling.

"Maybe," Leon admitted. "I mean, I figured if *you* could ask Sammie to go to the prom with you . . ."

"I keep telling you, dude. I didn't ask Sammie to go to the prom *with* me . . . we're just going to the prom *together*," Kevin said quickly.

"*What*-ever! Anyway, I was thinking that if *you* could go with a girl, maybe I could, too. Besides, what's the worst thing that could happen if I ask her?"

"Uhhh," Kevin said, pretending to think. "She could laugh in your face and call you a dork."

"Exactly!" Leon said. "Which would make it just another typical day for me at Medford Middle School."

The two friends cracked up and high-fived.

"I'm just busting your chops," Kevin said. "I'll bet Wendy says yes. She always laughs at your jokes in class. When are you going to ask her?"

"As soon as I can work up some courage, I guess," Leon said, flashing a nervous smile. "You probably won't believe this, but I don't have a lot of experience asking out girls."

"Me neither," Kevin admitted. "I guess you just, y'know, do it. I mean, that's what I did with Sammie. I just asked her if she wanted to go."

"Yeah? I thought that it wasn't a date."

"It's not. Well, not really."

"What's wrong? I thought you liked her," Leon said.

"I do," Kevin answered. "But I like her as a friend. Like I like you and Nicky and Timmy."

"Yeah, but you wouldn't ask any of *us* to go to the prom with you."

"I know, I know," Kevin said. "I just thought it would be fun if we all went and hung out with Timmy and his date. I mean, what's the big deal?"

"Are you sure Sammie knows you're just going as buddies?"

"Oh yeah. I mean, we hang out together all the time," Kevin said. "The only difference here is we'll be dressed up and there's going to be music."

While they had been talking, they arrived at the entrance to the school. With almost identical sighs, they started inside.

"See you at lunch," Leon said, and he disappeared into the sea of kids swarming along the main corridor.

"Later," Kevin said, and joined the flow of students hurrying up the stairs on their way to homeroom.

"Hey, Keller!"

The shout came from behind him, the voice cutting through the loud hum of chatter filling the stairwell and making Kevin wince.

*Elliot Kingman!*

He couldn't believe it. Was the new week going to start as badly as the one just past, and for the same reason? The thought made his heart sink, but he kept walking up the stairs. Maybe if he pretended not to hear him, he could get to the safety of his homeroom and . . .

But a sharp tug on his backpack made him cry out in alarm and grab for the handrail to keep from tumbling backward down the stairs.

"I'm talking to you, Keller!" Elliot snapped, this time in his ear.

Kevin turned around to find Elliot, standing two steps below him but still almost in his face. The bigger boy was angry.

"What do you want, Elliot?" Kevin asked, trying not to stammer.

"You got me in a lot of trouble, you little weasel," Elliot snarled.

"Me? What did I . . . ?"

"You can stop playing dumb, dummy. Roger saw you talking to old man Teitelbaum," Elliot said, moving up one step so that he now loomed menacingly over Kevin.

All around them, dozens of kids just kept moving up the stairs, rushing past them, hardly giving them a glance as they hurried to their classes.

Kevin never felt so alone in all his life.

"I didn't say anything to Mr. Teitelbaum! It was just a . . . a coincidence. He was leaving and heard . . ." Kevin said, unable to keep the whining tone from his voice.

"Yeah, right!" Elliot snapped. He poked a

finger into Kevin's chest, jabbing him hard as he spoke. "They called my parents and gave me a week of detention because of you, dork, so I can't do anything about it right now. But you better watch your back, hear me? 'Cause when you least expect it—payback!"

With one last savage poke, Elliot shoved roughly past Kevin and was swallowed up by the crowd.

Kevin stayed where he was, rubbing his chest and miserably realizing how wrong he had been a moment ago.

*Now* was the most alone he had ever felt!

● ● ●

"He's staring at you again," Nicky whispered across the table, looking quickly over Kevin's shoulder and then ducking his head.

Kevin took a bite out of his turkey sandwich and shrugged.

"It's a free country," he said. "He can look wherever he wants."

"Doesn't it make you nervous?" Leon asked, also in a whisper.

"Why are you guys whispering?" Kevin said. "He's all the way over on the other side of the cafeteria. He can't hear you."

"I can't believe you're not scared. *I* am, and I'm not even you," Nicky said.

But the truth was, Kevin was very unnerved by the campaign of intimidation that Elliot had been waging against him for the last couple of days. It seemed that everywhere in school he went, every time he turned a corner, Elliot was there, glaring at him with undisguised hatred. The lacrosse team captain hadn't said a word or made a threatening move against him since their encounter on the staircase Monday morning. He just stared, a constant reminder of the "payback" he had planned for Kevin.

"That Elliot Kingman makes me sick," Sammie said, shaking her head in disgust. "He acts like he owns this school and everybody in it."

"He might not own it, but he sure has a long-term lease on Kevin's butt," Leon said.

"Shut up, Leon," Sammie said. "I think Kevin's doing the mature thing by ignoring him."

"Let's *all* ignore him. Or at least stop talking about him, okay?" Kevin pleaded.

"Dude, the whole school's talking about it.

Elliot's telling everybody that he's waiting until his detention's over and then he's gonna make you pay," Nicky said. "You can't just sit around and wait for him to get you."

"What am I supposed to do? Hide under my bed until he graduates? Besides, he's only doing this to scare me so he can watch me squirm."

"You trying to tell us you're *not* squirming?" Leon said.

"Sure I am. Inside," Kevin said with a sudden grin. "But I'm not gonna let *him* see me do it."

"Good for you, Kevin," Sammie said.

"So what are you gonna do when he *does* come after you, man?" Nicky asked.

Kevin thoughtfully chewed a bite of turkey sandwich and said, "Well, I figure I'll bust up his knuckles good with my teeth and then bleed all over his shirt."

"Hey, that's pretty funny." Leon laughed and shoved his glasses up his nose.

Mercifully, the conversation then turned to other topics and Kevin could stop talking about Elliot for the moment.

But he couldn't stop thinking about him.

He had learned by being the new kid in so many schools that school bullies were mostly talk. He found that if he ignored them and kept out of their way, they usually grew tired of picking on him and moved on to other targets. While that didn't solve the bullying problem, it did take care of it for Kevin for the time being.

Until the next school.

Speaking of "other targets," Kevin looked around the cafeteria for Elliot's other main victim, Luke McPhee. He finally spotted him, sitting alone as usual, at a corner table with his head down, shoveling lunch into his mouth like he was in a race.

Poor guy, Kevin thought. As much as they thought of themselves as outsiders, at least the Geek Squad had each other. Luke, on the other hand, was a total loner. Kevin had never seen Luke in the company of any other kids, or even heard him utter a word out loud in either of the two classes they shared.

Kevin glanced behind him. Elliot was at his usual table, with the usual group of friends, acting, as Sammie had said, like they owned the school. As usual.

Kevin stood up.

"Where you going?" Nicky asked.

"I'll be right back," Kevin said.

Kevin walked across the lunchroom to Luke's table and stopped in front of it.

"Hey," Kevin said. "You're Luke, right?"

Luke was hunched over his lunch tray, his tangle of long brown hair hanging like a curtain over his face as he devoured a plate of mac and cheese. He raised his head just enough to be able to turn a sullen glance up at Kevin, but he said nothing.

"Hi. I'm Kevin Keller. My friends and I were wondering if you wanted to sit with us?"

Luke's forehead creased into a frown, almost as if he didn't understand the question.

"I mean, I saw you eating alone," Kevin said, trying a smile. "We thought maybe you'd like some company."

Luke shook his head.

"I'm okay," he said in a low voice, his words a monotone. Then he lowered his head back down to his plate and continued eating as though Kevin wasn't there.

"Oh. Yeah, that's cool. But if you ever, like, change your mind, just come on over, okay?" Kevin said, trying to keep his tone light and friendly despite his surprise.

Luke's head moved a few millimeters up and down in what he assumed to be a nod, and, after a few moments of awkwardly waiting for a further response, Kevin turned and went back to rejoin his friends.

"What was *that* all about?" Leon asked.

"Nothing," Kevin said. "I just asked him if he wanted to sit with us."

The others exchanged confused looks.

"*And* . . . ?" Nicky demanded.

Kevin shrugged. "And nothing."

"Yeah, but what did he say? I mean, can he even talk? I haven't heard him say a word since, like, fourth grade," Nicky said.

"He said he was okay," Kevin replied.

"That's it?"

"Yep. Two words: 'I'm okay.'"

"What a weirdo," Leon said, looking over at Luke and shaking his head.

"I don't think he's weird," Sammie said. "I think he's sad."

Kevin looked at Luke, then turned to glance at Elliot. The other boy was staring at him still, but a confused frown had, for the moment, replaced the menacing glare. He realized that others were looking at him strangely as well, all wondering why he had bothered speaking to the reclusive Luke McPhee.

"Me too," Kevin said softly.

# Chapter 6

Kevin and Sammie had English class the period after lunch. On the way, they stopped at his locker to pick up a textbook when Timmy Baker and Gail Rollins turned the corner and headed down the corridor in their direction.

Timmy leaned close to Gail and spoke into her ear. The pretty girl smiled and nodded, then continued on alone to her class. She didn't bother to look in Sammie or Kevin's direction as she passed.

"Hey, Kevin. Hi, Sammie," Timmy said.

"Hi," Sammie said.

"How's it going, Timmy?" Kevin said, smiling broadly.

"You tell me, man." The other boy chuckled as he leaned against the lockers. "You're the one everybody's been talking about the last couple of days."

"Oh. That." Kevin slammed shut his locker door and twirled the combination dial. "Elliot thinks I told on him for picking on Luke McPhee. I guess he's planning to pummel me as soon as he gets the chance."

"Kingman's a jerk," Timmy said. "He gets in trouble for something he's done and then looks for someone else to blame. I've known him my whole life and he's always been like that."

"Fat lot of good knowing that's gonna do me when the pummeling starts." Kevin sighed.

"Well, you're not really helping yourself with Elliot by hanging out with McPhee, you know," Timmy said.

"What're you talking about? When was I hanging out with Luke?"

Timmy shrugged, his eyes wandering over the passing students.

"I heard you were talking to him during lunch," he said.

Kevin shook his head in disbelief. "I don't believe it. I mean, I did *try* to talk him, but he totally wasn't interested."

"I'm just telling you what I hear, man," Timmy said.

"Yeah, thanks," Kevin said. "Anyway, how are those prom tickets selling since we put up the posters at the mall?"

"A lot better. Thanks again for helping me hang those. I really appreciate it."

Kevin grinned. "No problem. I mean, that's what friends do, right? And it'll be cool to hang out with you and . . ."

"Right," Timmy said, straightening up suddenly. "Hey, I better get to class."

"Okay. You going to be at the comic shop this afternoon?" Kevin said as Timmy started to walk away.

Timmy looked up the corridor, over Kevin's shoulder, and said quickly, "Um, no, not this week. We've got, uh, swim practice all afternoon. See you."

Kevin watched as Timmy hurried over to a group of boys from the swim team. He blended right in with them, laughing and high-fiving, grabbing one of his teammates in a playful headlock as they went off to class. Once again, Kevin marveled that a kid as popular as Timmy would also be friends with the Geek Squad. The thought brought a big grin to his face.

"He is such a cool guy," Kevin said.

"Sure," Sammie said in an icy tone of voice that Kevin was too distracted to notice. "Cool."

●●●

"... And so, why do you think Atticus Finch risked his life and reputation to defend Tom Robinson, both from an angry mob and in the courtroom, even though the entire town believed he was guilty?" Mr. Gallagher said from the front of the classroom. In his hand he held a copy of the book they had begun reading that week, *To Kill a Mockingbird* by Harper Lee.

Kevin had read the assigned classic novel with fascination, finishing it in just a few marathon sessions, the last taking him late into the night. When he had first brought it home, his mother told him it was one of her favorite books of all time, so for once she turned a blind eye to his staying up beyond his bedtime to read.

His was one of the first hands that shot up in response to Mr. Gallagher's question. The friendly, redheaded English teacher smiled and called on him.

"Because it was the right thing to do. The law says that everybody is innocent until proven guilty and that they're guaranteed a trial by a jury of their peers," Kevin said.

"But this story takes place when an African American couldn't count on fair treatment, not even from the law," Mr. Gallagher pointed out. "Atticus Finch may have been right in a strictly legal sense, but as far as the rest of the town was concerned, he was on the absolute wrong side of the issue where common practice was concerned."

"But that shouldn't matter," Kevin said. "Right is right, even if everybody else is telling you it's wrong."

"Yeah, but if everybody else thinks something is right, how do you know you're not the one who's getting it wrong?" a girl on the other side of the room asked.

"Because doing the right thing's not a matter of opinion," Sammie said.

"That's right," another boy said. "And I'll bet if Tom Robinson had been white and the girl he was accused of attacking had been African American, there probably wouldn't even have been a trial."

"And assuming someone's guilt or innocence or their worth as a human being based solely on the color of their skin, their religion, or any other reason is wrong no matter what,"

Mr. Gallagher said. "Atticus Finch knew that, and he knew that even if he was the only one standing up for what was right, he had to do it to prevent an injustice from being done."

Mr. Gallagher turned to the white board and wrote down a name.

Turning back to the class, he said, "Edmund Burke. You've probably never heard of him, but he was an eighteenth century Irish statesman and philosopher who once said, 'All that is necessary for evil to triumph is for good men to do nothing.' Atticus, you see, is a living example of this idea, a good man who tries to keep the racism of the townspeople from triumphing over law and justice, even at the risk of his own safety."

The lesson turned into a lively free-for-all as the kids shouted out thoughts and arguments. Mr. Gallagher acted as the moderator, keeping the discussion on topic, but other than that he let the students have their say. Practically the entire class joined in, except, Kevin noticed, Luke McPhee.

As usual, Luke kept to himself in his seat at the rear of the room. Now and then during the period, Kevin glanced over at Luke. The other boy was always slumped in his chair, arms folded across his chest, not moving except for his eyes, which darted from speaker to speaker from under his lowered brow.

What was Luke so angry about, Kevin wondered?

While the classroom discussion was about the characters of Atticus Finch and his children, Scout and Jem, Kevin couldn't help but think about Boo Radley, their mysterious neighbor in the book. Luke kept to himself and avoided contact with his classmates, like Boo, who stayed hidden from sight inside his house. Boo was kind of like a ghost haunting the lives of the Finch children and the story. Luke was a ghost, too, haunting Medford Middle School.

The difference was, while Boo tried reaching out to make a connection with people, Luke wouldn't. Or couldn't? Kevin knew what it was like not to have any friends. This was the seventh school he had attended since kindergarten and he hadn't always been lucky enough to find friends like Leon, Nicky, Sammie, and Timmy. Sitting alone at lunch, having no one to play with at recess or to hang out with after school, made you feel miserable.

He couldn't imagine anyone *choosing* to live like that.

But when he tried reaching out to the other boy, Luke didn't want anything to do with him. He couldn't force his friendship on Luke.

Could he?

Kevin figured there was only one way to find out.

# Chapter 7

"What'd you mean you're not coming with us to the mall? It's new comic book day!" Leon cried in shock. "Can't you hear the new releases calling your name from Comics Universe?"

"I'm not skipping out on you, I just said I'd meet you there later," Kevin said. "There's something I've got to do first."

"What've you got to do that's more important than the comic shop?" Nicky asked in disbelief.

"Just . . . something," Kevin said.

The three boys were standing in front of the middle school after the dismissal bell.

"But we always go together. It's like . . . a tradition!" Leon said.

"Yeah. Who am I supposed to make fun of Leon with if you're not there?" Nicky asked.

Kevin was looking around at the rest of the kids rushing out of the school, some to the line of cars driven by waiting parents, others to their assigned school buses, and many more to walk home along the crowded streets. Most everyone was with somebody else, in pairs or groups of three or more.

Everyone except Luke McPhee.

He slunk out of school by himself, hunched under the weight of his backpack, his head down. He didn't look at anybody else, just at the ground and his own two feet.

"Look, I gotta go. Catch you later, I promise, okay?" Kevin said, and he raced off.

"Where is he going?" Leon asked in exasperation.

"I dunno. Want to follow him?" Nicky asked.

"Yeah, I would," Leon said. "Except it's new comic book day."

"Yeah," Nicky agreed.

The friends exchanged shrugs and turned to start the walk to the mall.

● ● ●

Kevin had never followed anyone before, so Luke was proving to be the perfect subject for his first try.

Luke looked neither right nor left, nor at anyone or anyplace he passed on the long walk up Main Street. He just kept his head down and plowed right on, as if he were the only person in the world. He paid no attention to his surroundings. Kevin was pretty sure he could have walked right up alongside the other boy and Luke still wouldn't have noticed him. But just in case Luke did decide to look up, Kevin kept about a block behind the other boy and used whatever cover he could find to stay out of sight.

For the first few blocks, Kevin couldn't deny that what he was doing was sort of fun. In his imagination, he pretended he was a spy on a top secret mission, trailing an enemy operative to his hidden lair. Sure, it was a dangerous job, but Agent Keller was the man for the task!

But, after twenty minutes, the fun was wearing off and he was starting to wonder if Luke was even on his way home. Most kids who lived this far from the school rode the bus or were driven by their parents. Who knew where this mysterious, silent boy went after classes were over?

Kevin's plan had been to follow him home and try to talk to him there, away from the prying eyes of the rest of the school. And, after Timmy's earlier warning about his being seen with Luke, a little part of him felt it was probably better that if they did talk, it was someplace where Elliot wouldn't find out . . . but that wasn't a part of which he was very proud.

A few minutes later, Luke finally turned off Main Street, onto Taylor Road. Kevin wasn't familiar with this part of town. He mostly knew his own neighborhood and a few surrounding areas where his friends lived. The houses they passed reminded him of the ones on his own street. They were all well kept, with freshly painted shingles or bright, clean siding, and neat green lawns and flowering gardens behind picket fences, new-model cars parked in some of the driveways.

But Luke didn't turn up a path to any of these houses. He kept on walking, making another turn a couple blocks later, and one more several streets after that. With fewer places to duck out of sight in this residential area, Kevin had fallen a little farther behind Luke, but he needn't have worried. The other boy remained unaware of anything but his own two feet.

With every passing block, the houses and lawns seemed to get a little smaller and a little shabbier. The concrete sidewalks were cracked, and the cars parked at the curb were not quite as new.

Kevin was well aware that some kids lived in neighborhoods nicer than his while others were from less well-to-do circumstances. It never mattered to him how much money his friends' parents made or what streets their homes were on. He didn't care that Nicky DeMarco wore hand-me-downs and lived in a crowded flat just blocks away from the train tracks. It also made no difference that Sammie Warren's dad was the president of the company where Nicky's dad worked as a maintenance man, just like it wouldn't have mattered to them if his father had been a bus driver instead of a colonel in the United States Army. What mattered about a person was how they treated those around them and what was in their hearts.

And that's what Kevin had hoped to learn when he followed Luke home. He wasn't interested in making a judgment about his address.

But when Luke finally reached home, it was hard for Kevin not to form an opinion.

Maple Lane was a dead-end street lined

with a dozen small houses and ending at a rusting, sagging chain-link fence that was overgrown with creeping weeds and vines. On the other side of the fence was the parking lot for an abandoned factory complex.

While many of the houses on the street could have used some repairs or a fresh coat of paint, they were all being cared for as well as they could be by their owners. Lawns were clipped, bushes and hedges were trimmed, and trash cans were stored neatly alongside the drives.

But not the house Luke entered.

It looked sad and neglected, a lot like Luke himself. Green paint peeled from its weathered shingles, and shutters hung crookedly beside the windows, one of which was covered by a raggedly cut sheet of plywood that was rippled with age. The screen door had come off its hinges and was leaning against the wall next to the front door, and it had probably been a couple of months since the small front lawn had seen the attention of a mower blade. The once-white picket fence that faced the street had started to tumble over and was propped up against two overflowing metal trash cans.

Kevin watched from the corner, nervously biting his lip. He really had intended to talk to Luke, but the sight of that house made him pause.

He hadn't really thought about what he would find when he got there, but this sure as heck wasn't it. He wondered if this was why Luke took the long walk to and from school every day instead of riding the bus. He was ashamed for anyone to see where he lived.

If a kid ever needed a friend, it was Luke McPhee, but Kevin was no longer sure coming to his house was such a good idea. If Luke knew that Kevin knew, he might be embarrassed and reject his offer of friendship.

On the other hand, maybe if Luke saw it didn't make any difference to him, he would be cool with it.

Kevin wasn't aware how long he stood there debating with himself over what to do before the door to Luke's house flew open and Luke came running out. Kevin heard the muffled sound of an angry adult voice, a shout chasing after Luke into the street, but he couldn't make out what was being said.

But he did hear Luke's response, an angry

sob: "Why can't you just leave me alone? I hate you! I wish we were all dead!"

Suddenly, Kevin's mind was made up for him. Luke was tearing up the street straight for where he stood. If he were caught spying on him, Luke would *never* want to have anything to do with Kevin.

He turned and ran.

●●●

Kevin found his way back to Main Street and got on the downtown bus to the mall. The whole time, Luke's words were ringing in his ears.

*I hate you! I wish we were all dead!*

Maybe trying to befriend the troubled boy was too big a project for him. He understood unhappiness and he even knew what it was like to be angry, but not like that. No matter how bad things had gotten, he had never wished harm to anybody . . . not even bullies like Elliot who made his life miserable.

But at the end of the day, Kevin went home to a loving, supportive family. Sure, it hurt his feelings when kids made fun of him because of his weight or complexion, but he had a mother and father who made it clear to him that those were just temporary imperfections, not anything that defined him as a person. Eventually, he would lose the extra weight, his skin would clear up, and the braces would come off his teeth. What mattered was who he was inside.

But what if, after being picked on by guys like Elliot all day, he had to go home to a place where the people who were supposed to protect him from hurt turned out to be just as big a bunch of bullies as the ones in school?

Kevin was still debating with himself over what he should do when he got to the mall. He stopped in at Comics Universe and quickly scanned the racks for the new releases. He was so distracted that he would have skipped the latest issue of *The Black Hood* if Mr. Salerno hadn't pointed it out to him.

As he waited for his change, the door opened and, glancing up, he saw Timmy Baker walk in.

Timmy saw him at the same time and paused in surprise. Then he smiled and continued in, the pretty, brown-haired Gail Rollins right behind him.

"Hi, Kevin," Timmy said. He pointed to the bag of comics in his hands. "Uh . . . anything good this week?"

"Hey," Kevin said. "Er, yeah. *The Black Hood* and a new *Web* graphic novel."

"Great. That's cool. I gotta pick those up," Timmy said with an uncomfortable grin.

"Is this going to take long, Timmy? We were supposed to meet everyone five minutes ago," Gail interrupted, looking around the comic shop with distaste.

"So . . . I guess swim practice was canceled, huh?" Kevin said with a frown as he accepted his change from Mr. Salerno.

Timmy shrugged. "Oh. Yeah, Coach canceled at the last minute."

"Since when do you ever have practice on Wednesday?" Gail said.

"It . . . it was a special practice," Timmy said quickly to her. He smiled at Kevin. "I thought you guys were usually here earlier."

"Yeah, we are, but there was something I had to do first," Kevin said.

"Let's go, Timmy," Gail said impatiently.

The dark-haired boy shrugged and said, "Okay, Gail. I gotta split, Kevin. See you."

"Sure," Kevin said. He smiled at Gail. "See you at the prom!"

"You will?" she said in surprise as Timmy took her by the hand and hurried to the comic rack where he busied himself picking out the new books. Gail took out her cell phone and, with an amused glance at Kevin, started texting.

Kevin said good-bye to Mr. Salerno and left to find his friends.

# Chapter 8

Seeing Timmy at Comics Universe wasn't the only surprise Kevin got that afternoon at the mall.

His next stop was Dunk-A-Muffin, where he expected to find Leon, Nicky, and Sammie at their regular spot, reading comics and eating donuts. They were there and they had their donuts, but there were two new faces at the table with them.

The first was Wendy Butler, the girl Leon had earlier hinted he might ask to the prom. She was a smiling, round-faced girl with jet-black hair that she wore pulled back in a ponytail, and who dressed in blue jeans, high-top sneakers, and oversize black T-shirts featuring rock bands. She worked on the middle school newspaper, the *Medford Monitor*, and wrote in a light, breezy style that reflected her easygoing manner.

The other was Cheryl Abrams, a tall, thin

girl with an unruly mop of curly red hair, a face full of freckles, and bright blue eyes that were constantly on the lookout for an interesting moment to capture with her ever-present camera, which Cheryl employed as the photographer for the *Monitor*. Shy and reserved, Cheryl wore drab brown or khaki-colored shirts and skirts, as though her hair called enough attention to her.

The kids made room for Kevin at the table while he bought his customary chocolate-frosted donuts and iced tea. When he returned to take his seat, everybody was laughing at Leon, who was in the middle of telling a joke.

"So the man goes out back where the dog the woman wants to sell is and says to him, 'Your owner claims you can talk, but I don't believe it.' The dog answers, 'But it's true, I can talk.' The man is amazed and says, 'Wow! So what's your story?' And the dog says, 'Well, after they learned I could talk, I went to work as a spy for the government, eavesdropping on enemy agents. After that, I was undercover for the police and helped break up the mob.'

"The man is so impressed, he runs back to the owner and says, 'That dog is incredible. I have to have him. How much do you want?' 'Ten dollars,' the owner says. 'Ten dollars? For a talking dog? Why are you selling him so cheap?' The woman tells him, 'Because he's such a liar! He never did *any* of that stuff!'"

"That is so funny." Wendy giggled. "You always have the best jokes, Leon."

"Thanks," Leon said, ducking down to take a bite of his donut so she wouldn't see him blush.

"Leon's the funniest guy in our grade," Kevin said, jumping in with a good word for his friend.

"I know. Sometimes I think I'm going to get into trouble for laughing so hard in class," Wendy added.

"So, Kevin, Sammie says you guys are going to the prom," Cheryl said.

"Uh-huh," he answered. "How about you?"

Wendy flicked a nervous glance in Leon's direction.

"Well, sort of. I mean, we'll be there to cover the story for the *Monitor*," Wendy said. "But no one's, you know, asked me to go with them or anything."

Kevin glanced at Leon. He looked scared out of his wits. This was the first time Kevin could ever remember seeing the other boy at a loss for words in front of an audience.

Even though Kevin hadn't told her that Leon was interested in the girl reporter, Sammie just seemed to pick up on what was going on.

"You know what would be cool?" Sammie said. "If we all went to the prom together."

"Yeah!" Nicky blurted out, spraying donut crumbs across the table.

Everyone started to laugh, even the petrified Leon.

"Oops!" Nicky said, quickly wiping his mouth with a napkin. "Sorry. But I was thinking . . ."

"Well, that's a first," Leon said, with a smile of gratitude aimed at Sammie.

"Ha-ha! Um, anyway, I was saying, uh . . . Cheryl, maybe I could . . . I mean, you don't live that far from me . . . so, you know, if my dad's gonna drive me, maybe I could pick you up since it's on the way . . . or something . . . if you wanna . . ." Nicky stammered.

Cheryl blushed. For a moment it looked like all her freckles had blended together into matching scarlet patches on her pale cheeks.

"S-sure, Nicky," she said in a soft voice. "I think that would be nice."

Wendy looked at Leon with an expectant smile.

"I guess that just leaves us without dates, huh?" she said.

"Uh, I guess. Unless, y'know . . . ?" he said, shrugging.

Wendy's smile grew wider. "Thank you, Leon. I'd love to."

Kevin couldn't believe it. Just like that, the Geek Squad all had dates to the prom!

Maybe it wasn't such a bad day after all.

●●●

Later, as they were leaving the mall to go home, Kevin couldn't stop talking about their friends and the upcoming prom.

"This is gonna be so cool," he said. "Remember last week, when Timmy told the guys they should get dates themselves? They didn't think that was *ever* going to happen, but now we can all go together. That was a great idea, Sammie."

"Thanks," Sammie said. "I could see Wendy and Cheryl wanted to be asked, so I just gave Leon and Nicky a little push in the right direction."

"Man, I can hardly wait to tell Timmy," he said with a big smile.

She looked at him with a frown.

"Why?" she asked. "You *do* know he's going to be hanging out with his friends, right?"

"Sure. And we're his friends, too," Kevin said.

Sammie stopped in her tracks.

"I . . . I'm not so sure about that, Kevin."

"What are you talking about? Of course we are. I mean, he sometimes sits with us at lunch, doesn't he? And he's always coming to the mall to hang out at the comic shop and Dunk-A-Muffin and stuff."

"I know, but the only time he sits with us is when none of his swim-team buddies are around. And he never comes *with* us to Comics Universe. He only meets us there."

"So what?"

"So," she said gently, "everybody from school hangs out at the mall and he doesn't want to take the chance that his friends will see him with us."

"You're crazy," Kevin said hotly. "Timmy's my friend. Maybe *you* don't like him for some reason, but he's always nice to us . . ."

"I'm not saying he's not, but that doesn't make him a real friend."

"Oh yeah? Name one thing he's done that makes you say that?" he demanded.

"Please, don't be so angry, Kevin. But don't you see he never wants you around when he's with the cool kids or his girlfriend? I'm just trying to warn you . . ."

"There's nothing I need to be warned about and I don't understand why you're saying this stuff about Timmy. You know, I wouldn't even have asked you to the prom if it wasn't for him."

Sammie gasped and looked at Kevin, her eyes wide with hurt. He realized at once that he had gone too far.

"I . . . I'm sorry, Sammie," he said quickly. "That's not true, really! You're my best friend, you know that."

She swallowed hard and nodded, but he could see she was fighting back tears.

"I know," she said softly. "And I'm not trying to pick on Timmy, Kevin. I don't want you to get hurt, that's all. I mean, while we were waiting for you before at Dunk-A-Muffin, I saw Timmy and Gail coming out of Jimmy's Rocketship.

He didn't have practice, like he told you this morning."

"I know," Kevin said. "I saw him at the comic shop. He said the coach had canceled practice. What's the big deal?"

"Mr. Krueger is also the advisor for the nature club. It meets every Wednesday, so he never schedules *any* team practices for then."

Kevin shook his head.

"You're wrong about Timmy, okay?" he said firmly.

He turned and started to walk quickly toward the exit.

"Kevin . . . ?" Sammie called after him.

"I'll see you tomorrow," he called back over his shoulder and shoved his way through the doors. It took several deep breaths to calm himself down, and as he turned to start the walk home, he wondered why what Sammie told him had made him so upset.

# Chapter 9

As soon as he got home, Kevin changed his clothes and went out for a run. He had promised his father he would try to keep to a regular routine and build up his endurance.

"It's okay that you're not into sports, but everyone needs to get some sort of exercise to stay healthy," Colonel Keller told him. "And the best part about running is, you can do it anywhere and you've always got all the equipment you need with you right there at the end of your legs."

He had to admit he really didn't mind it so much. He was able to run at his own pace, and while the first couple of times he went out on his own he listened to music on his MP3 player, he had forgotten to charge it the next time and discovered that he actually preferred running without it. The peace and quiet gave him a chance to think, and with his mind able to wander, he didn't focus on the running, which allowed him to go even farther.

On this run, he had plenty of thoughts to distract him.

He wasn't angry at Sammie, but he couldn't point to what it was that had made him so mad. There was no doubt in his mind that he and Timmy were friends. He had a lot of things in common with the tall, handsome boy, from comics to music to favorite TV programs. Whenever they hung out, they had plenty to talk about and Timmy obviously respected his opinions. Wasn't he always asking Kevin for recommendations of comics he should read?

So what if the swimmer had another group of friends who didn't overlap with the Geek Squad? Maybe it was just that the rest of them weren't as nice as Timmy. True, it was a small number of kids, like Elliot and his pals, who actually went out of their way to be cruel, but the majority just ignored kids like Kevin and Nicky, and that was almost as hurtful as the bullying. Maybe Timmy didn't include them in all parts of his life, but who said he had to?

Kevin felt a lot better by the time he was nearing the end of his run. He still didn't quite understand where Sammie was coming from, but he decided he'd just have to chalk it up as a "girl thing." He had heard his mother say more than once that "men are from Mars, and women are from Venus," and while he wasn't sure he understood *exactly* what that meant, he got that it had something to do with the way the opposite sexes thought and reacted to things. Anyway, just because Sammie had a problem with Timmy didn't mean Kevin had to agree with her.

He was still a couple of blocks from home when he passed Becky Sherman's house on Eden Drive. Becky was in Gail Rollins's clique and was a cheer-squad star who always seemed to travel in a pack with the other popular girls, more often than not trailed by boys from the different teams. This afternoon, Becky and some of her girlfriends were hanging out on her front porch when Kevin ran by.

Seeing him, she jumped to her feet and started to wave, calling out in a singsong voice, "Hiya, Kevin Keller! See you at the prom!"

The other girls all started to laugh, some doubling over with hysterical giggles.

Kevin didn't know what was so funny about that.

But he did know when he was being made the butt of a cruel joke. His face hot with the all-too-familiar burn of humiliation, he picked up speed and kept running, but not fast enough to escape the girls' laughter.

●●●

After dinner, Kevin went to his room to do his homework, but as hard as he tried he couldn't get the sound of Becky Sherman and her friends' laughter out of his head. It was usually easy to figure out what they were making fun of . . . he was overweight, had zits, wore braces, didn't play sports, and collected comic books. Any one of those was enough ammunition, even for kids with little or no imagination. But what was it about his going to the prom that was so hysterically funny to those girls?

He tried to put it out of his mind and get through his math homework. Algebra, at least, made sense to him, and numbers always did what they were supposed to do. Not like people. He was beginning to think he didn't understand people at all, not even his friends. Probably not even himself.

"Hey, pal," Colonel Keller said, poking his

head in the door. "You busy?"

Kevin looked up from his textbook and realized he had been staring at the same problem for the last fifteen minutes.

"Hey, Dad," he said. "No, I was just doing my homework."

His father stepped into the room, his hands in the pockets of his neatly pressed khakis.

"Anything I can help you with? You look pretty confused there."

Kevin shook his head and leaned back in his chair.

"Naw. I mean, I get the math. I guess I've got other things on my mind."

"Such as . . . ?"

Kevin folded his arms and sighed. "Just stuff. You know the prom is coming up, right?"

"Sure. I read about it in the PTA newsletter," Colonel Keller said. "You know, you don't need to have a date to go. It's really all right for you and your friends to go stag. A lot of guys . . ."

"Oh no," Kevin interrupted. "I've got a date. At least, I'm going with Sammie Warren."

"You are?" his father said, a pleased smile spreading across his face. "Well, that's great. So what's the problem?"

"I don't know," Kevin said miserably. "It's just that no matter what I do . . . I just don't seem to be able to fit in, Dad."

"In what way, Kev? I know you've made friends and you have a date for the prom. It sounds like you're doing okay," his father said.

"I do . . . I am . . . but only sort of. I mean, the only kids who want to be friends with me are the *other* freaks and geeks. Everybody else just ignores us or laughs at us," Kevin said.

"What about the Baker boy? You said he's one of the most popular kids in school and he's friendly with you," Colonel Keller said with a concerned frown.

"I guess," Kevin replied. "But Timmy's different . . . we like a lot of the same stuff, but he's so busy with the swim team and other things, he doesn't have a lot of time to hang out with us."

His father squeezed Kevin's shoulder and said, "I know it's difficult, kiddo. You never have a chance to stay in one place long enough for people to get to know you very well."

"They know me," Kevin grumbled. "They just don't like me."

Colonel Keller squatted next to Kevin's chair.

"No. If they really *did* know you, they would like you. You're a good guy, Kevin, but you march to your own drummer. Unfortunately, you're at an age when everybody feels like they have to be just like everybody else or they don't fit in. Anybody who's even a little different is treated like an outsider."

"But *I* don't treat anybody like that," Kevin said, thinking about Luke McPhee. "What's the point of being mean to someone just because they're different? I mean, aren't those the kids who need friends the most?"

Colonel Keller smiled and patted Kevin's shoulder. "You're right, kiddo. I'm proud of you for seeing that. But all you can do is be who you are and just hope the rest of the world catches up with you one of these days."

Kevin tried his best to smile and picked up his pencil.

"Thanks, Dad. Anyway, I better finish my homework."

His father smiled back and plucked the pencil from his hand. "You can't fool me. You're just going to go back to staring at the page. I think you need to blow off a little steam first to help you concentrate."

"Really, Dad, I'm fine. I already went for a run before . . ."

"Come on," Colonel Keller said. "There's another judo throw I want to show you. It will just take ten minutes."

"Okay," Kevin said in surrender. "Boy, most dads make their kids finish their homework *before* they get to play."

"I'm not 'most dads,' kiddo," Colonel Keller said with an amused twinkle in his eyes.

"No, sir, you're not," Kevin agreed as he pushed his chair back from his desk. "Thank goodness for that!"

# Chapter 10

*"See you at the prom!"*

From the moment he arrived at school the next morning, Kevin was greeted by giggling girls repeating that to him. They called it out as he walked through the doors, said it when they passed him in the hall, whispered it as he sat in class, and sang it out to him in chorus across the gym. Girls who had never given him a second look . . . girls he was surprised even knew his name, much less that he existed, were suddenly speaking to him. But only to say that and break up laughing with their friends.

*"See you at the prom!"*

"What's *that* all about?" Nicky whispered to him in third period social studies.

"I don't know, but they've been doing it all morning," Kevin said, scrunched down in his seat but unable to make himself small enough to disappear from view.

He tried his best to ignore them, but as the

morning progressed, it got harder and harder to pretend. By the time lunch rolled around, he was afraid to even go into the cafeteria. His stomach was so twisted up in knots by what was going on that he wasn't hungry anyway. Instead, he skipped lunch and went to hide out in the library.

The afternoon was, if possible, even worse. Everywhere he went, kids pointed and laughed, making him the punch line of their secret joke.

*"See you at the prom!"*

Kevin hurried through the day with his eyes down, afraid that at any moment he would burst into tears. The only thing keeping that from happening was his fear of being further humiliated in front of the whole school.

Whatever had triggered it, he could only hope that they would get bored with the taunts and that it would all be forgotten by tomorrow. He didn't think he could take another day like this.

When the dismissal bell rang, Kevin was one of the first kids out the door, hoping to outrun any more mocking voices. All he wanted was to get as far away from Medford Middle School and its students as possible.

But he had one more hurdle to overcome before he got his wish.

Elliot Kingman.

The other boy was waiting outside, leaning against the flagpole. When he saw Kevin, he straightened up and, with a nasty grin on his face, stepped right into his path. Kevin tried to go around him, but Elliot just moved to block his way.

"Hey, Kevin Keller," Elliot said in a low, threatening tone. "See *you* at the prom!"

Kevin felt himself shaking, more from anger than fear. He didn't think anything the other boy did to him physically could be as painful as the day he had just endured.

"What do you want, Elliot?" Kevin asked.

"My detention's up after tomorrow, dweeb," Elliot said.

"I told you before, I didn't tell on you to Mr. Teitelbaum."

"Right. Just like I'm not gonna pound on you at the prom. Remember I told you payback was coming when you least expected it? Well, I changed my mind. I decided I *want* you to know when," Elliot said in an angry growl.

"Fine. You told me," Kevin said. He started

to brush past Elliot, but the other boy grabbed his arm.

"Oooh, pretty brave all of a sudden, aren't you, Keller?"

Kevin shook off his hand, trying to keep the quiver out of his voice as he snapped defiantly, "What're you gonna do, Elliot? Threaten me some more?"

"What's going on here?"

At the doorway, Mrs. Martinez, the assistant principal, stood frowning at them.

"Nothing, Mrs. Martinez," Elliot said. "Me and Kevin were just talking."

"You don't need to use your hands to talk to someone, Mr. Kingman. Aren't you supposed to be in detention?"

Elliot glared at Kevin as he nodded and said, "Yes, ma'am."

"Then get going," she ordered.

"I'm going," Elliot said. On his way in, he looked back at Kevin and added, "See you at the prom, Kevin."

"Is everything all right, Kevin?" Mrs. Martinez asked.

"Yeah," Kevin said. "I mean, yes, Mrs. Martinez. Everything's fine. Thanks."

Then he turned away and raced toward home.

●●●

Later that afternoon, Sammie, Leon, and Nicky appeared at Kevin's bedroom door.

"Your mom told us it was okay to come up," Nicky said.

"Yeah, we figured you wouldn't mind us interrupting homework," Leon said.

"We hardly saw you all day," Sammie said. "Where were you at lunch?"

Kevin stared at his notebook and shrugged.

"I wasn't hungry, so I went to the library instead," he said.

His three friends exchanged awkward glances.

"Dude, listen, we heard what was going on," Nicky said at last.

"The whole school heard," Kevin said softly. "I . . . I don't even know why they all think that's so funny."

"We do," Leon said. "Wendy overheard some of the girls talking about it in the bathroom and told us about it."

Kevin looked up. "Yeah? What did they say?"

"It was Gail Rollins's fault," Sammie said. "When you saw her and Timmy at the comic shop yesterday, did you say you'd see her at the prom?"

"Yeah. So . . . ?"

"So . . . she sent texts to all her friends and told them."

"Okay, but I still don't get what's so funny about that," Kevin said, confused.

"She . . . she thinks it's funny that *you* think she'll be hanging out with you at the prom," Sammie said. "I'm sorry, Kevin."

Kevin shook his head. "I can't believe Timmy's dating anyone who would do something that mean," he said.

"Yeah, well, I didn't hear Timmy telling anybody to stop." Sammy sniffed.

"Don't start that again, all right?" Kevin snapped. "Just because Gail did something creepy doesn't mean he agrees with her."

"Maybe not . . . but what about what we talked about in English class the other day? Remember that quote Mr. Gallagher gave us?" Sammie replied.

"Which quote?" Kevin said, even though he knew exactly what she was talking about.

"'All that is necessary for evil to triumph is for good men to do nothing,'" Sammie said. "Timmy may be a nice guy, but he didn't do anything when all his friends were making fun of you today."

"Yeah, well, neither did you!" Kevin barked angrily.

"There isn't anything we *can* do! Nobody listens to us," Sammie cried. "But Timmy could've told them to stop."

"Maybe he didn't hear . . . ?" Kevin said defensively.

"That's ridiculous. The whole grade knows about it. *Everybody* was laughing at you, Kevin!"

"You too, huh, Sammie? I bet you couldn't wait to tell me how crummy a friend Timmy is! I don't know why you're always so jealous of him!" Kevin shouted.

"Because sometimes it seems as if you like him more than you like me," Sammie shouted back, sounding miserable. Then she turned and ran out of the room.

Kevin watched her go, listening to her footsteps pounding down the stairs and then the front door slamming shut behind her.

"Dude!" Leon said in a voice barely above a whisper.

"Yeah, really!" Nicky added.

"I know, I know," Kevin groaned. "I'm a jerk. I'm totally evil."

"You're not evil, Kev . . . just stupid," Nicky said.

"Yeah. Sammie's, like, your second best friend . . . after me, that is," Leon said.

"You? What about me?" Nicky said, giving the other boy a dirty look.

"Fine, after *us*," Leon conceded.

Kevin leaned down and tugged on his sneakers.

"I gotta find her and apologize," he said.

"Want us to go with you?" Nicky asked.

"No. I think I better talk to her alone." Kevin finished tying up his shoes and got to his feet. "I'll see you guys later."

● ● ●

"Sammie's not here," Mrs. Warren told Kevin when she answered his knock at her door. "I thought she said she was going over to your house."

"Oh, I, um . . . wasn't home," Kevin said.

"Any idea where else she might have gone?"

"Well, if she's not with you or the other boys, she might be at the dog park. You know how she likes to go there and sketch the people and their pets sometimes."

Kevin thanked her and took off down the street. Waverly Park was a popular spot for dog owners in this part of Medford. The little park was fenced in and provided a safe area for dogs of all sizes to run off the leash and play together. Kevin knew that Sammie liked drawing the people and pets who frequented the park, often finding amazing similarities between humans and their canine companions that she was able to turn into funny little cartoons.

He entered through the park's single gate, making sure to close it behind him to prevent any dogs from accidentally getting out. Before he could take two steps, Kevin was greeted by a fluffy little tan Pomeranian and a barking beagle who raced up to sniff at his feet before running off to continue their play.

Kevin hurried toward the far end of the park, where big old shade trees hung over benches for dog owners to rest on while their dogs had their exercise. Sammie would usually park herself there with her sketch pad and colored pencils to draw, often giving the caricatures she did of the dogs to their delighted masters.

But while Sammie was nowhere to be seen, another of his classmates was. Luke McPhee sat in the shadows at the end of the farthest bench, bent over his notebook doing his homework.

Kevin stopped dead in his tracks. He hadn't really given much thought to Luke since he had followed him home the other day. And while he really did need to find Sammie, the stuff he had gone through today made him realize that this was how Luke must feel *every day* at school. At least Kevin had a few friends and two sympathetic parents to talk to when things got bad. Luke didn't have anyone.

"Hey, Luke," Kevin called as he approached the other boy.

Luke looked up, blinking in surprise when he saw Kevin.

"So, I've never seen you here before. Do you live close by?" Kevin asked with a smile.

"It's a public park. I come here all the time. Nobody bothers me," Luke said, and bent back over his work.

"Yeah, I know, I'm just saying, my friends

and I come here a lot and we've never seen you . . ."

Luke slammed shut his notebook and looked angrily at Kevin.

"What do you want? Why do you keep trying to talk to me?" the thin boy demanded.

"I . . . I'm just . . . I don't know," Kevin stammered in reply.

"I saw you following me home, too," he said harshly. "What's your problem?"

"No problem. I'm just trying to be friendly, that's all," Kevin said, suddenly defensive.

"Yeah? Why?"

"What'd you mean 'why'?"

"*Why* do you want to be my friend? Nobody else in Medford does," Luke said hotly.

"Well, I'm not *from* Medford," Kevin snapped.

Luke quickly started to gather up his books.

"If you were, maybe you'd know I just want to be left alone, okay?"

"Yeah, sure, okay," Kevin said. "And if this is the way you treat someone who's just trying to be nice, I guess you won't have any problem with that."

Luke hugged his schoolbooks to his chest and glared at Kevin.

"Kids tell me all sorts of stuff, but when I trust them even a little, I find out they were only doing it so they could prank me. *Why* should I trust you?" he said with a quiver in his voice.

Kevin stopped and forced himself to take a breath and calm down, but as he was doing that, Luke just shook his head and started to hurry away.

"Because . . . I *know* how you feel, Luke!" Kevin called after him.

Luke spun suddenly around, his chest heaving in anger and sadness as he screamed, "*Nobody* knows how I feel!"

"Then tell me," Kevin pleaded.

For a single second, a look of hope crossed Luke's face and Kevin thought he was going to give in and break down, but with a violent shake of his head, that moment was gone and Luke's features turned hard again.

"I can't," Luke said. "I can never tell anybody!"

And he ran off into the trees.

# Chapter 11

When Sammie went to her locker before first period the next morning, she found Kevin sitting on the floor next to it.

"Hi," he said.

"My mom told me you came by looking for me," she said.

"Yeah. I wanted to tell you I was sorry."

Sammie nodded and said, "Me too."

"You didn't do anything wrong," Kevin replied, getting to his feet.

"Yes, I did. I shouldn't keep talking trash about Timmy. I know he's your friend and you like him," she said.

"So are you, but I don't want to have to choose between you guys," Kevin told her.

"You won't have to, I promise."

Kevin smiled. "Thanks. He really *is* a good guy, and even if he doesn't like me as much as I like him, that's no reason for us to stop being friends. I mean, I know I'm never gonna be as cool or as good looking as him, but—"

"Okay, look," Sammie interrupted. "I'm just going to say this one last thing and then I'll shut up about it, okay?"

"Okay," Kevin said warily.

"You . . . and me, and Nicky, and even big-mouth Leon, we're *all* as good as anybody else in this school. I know I'm overweight and you have braces and Nicky wears old clothes, and we're all weird because we like comic books and know more about stupid science fiction TV shows than *anybody* needs to know, but none of that makes a difference. The only thing that really matters is what's in here." She pointed to her heart. "I know you guys would do anything to help me and you know I'd do anything for you, right?"

Kevin swallowed hard and nodded.

"So I don't care what anybody else at Medford thinks about me, and you shouldn't, either, just as long as our real friends think we're cool. And we do, Kev," Sammie said.

With that, she leaned close and kissed him on the cheek. He felt himself start to blush.

"See you at the prom!" Sammie said with a shy grin and laughing eyes.

Kevin smiled, happy he and Sammie had made up, but, for the second day in a row, also a little confused. Yesterday, his confusion had been caused by the taunt that had been hurled at him.

Today, it was caused by Sammie Warren.

●●●

As Kevin bent over the water fountain outside of English class to take a drink, a quiet voice behind him said, "Did you mean it?"

He looked up in surprise. Luke was standing on the other side of the hallway with his back up against the end of a row of lockers. His books were clutched to his chest and he was watching Kevin with wide, frightened eyes.

"Huh?" Kevin said, wiping his mouth.

"Did you mean it?" Luke repeated urgently. "About wanting to, y'know . . . to be friends?"

"Yeah, sure I did," Kevin nodded, crossing to join the other boy. "Hey, come over to my house after school. Me and the guys are just gonna play some video games and stuff, but you can hang out with us."

"I . . . I can't today. I've got to go home to

watch my little sister. This is one of the nights my dad works."

"Oh, okay." Kevin's face lit up with an idea. "I know what! Do you have a ticket to the prom? A bunch of us are going together. Come with us. It'll be fun."

Luke seemed to grow even more pale at the very thought and he shook his head.

"No, I can't . . . I mean . . . I don't have a ticket or . . . or the right clothes," he said. "Maybe this wasn't such a good idea . . ."

"No, it's cool," Kevin said. "Look, the dance is totally informal so it doesn't matter what you wear. And you can still get a ticket. They're selling them outside the gym all day."

But Kevin could see Luke was already retreating back into himself. Nicky and Leon had been in school with this lonely, sad boy their whole lives and neither of them could remember his having any friends since third or fourth grade. Maybe something had happened to make him afraid of friendships . . . or maybe he had just forgotten how it was done.

Whatever the reason, he could see Luke literally drawing back inside himself, hunching his shoulders and lowering his head as if to make himself smaller.

"I gotta go," he whispered, and before Kevin could stop him, he was gone.

● ● ●

When the morning proved to be free of a repeat of yesterday's taunting, Kevin decided to risk going to the cafeteria for lunch. He didn't know if the kids had just grown tired of teasing him or if the excitement of the upcoming prom had replaced it in their priorities. Whatever the reason, he was happy not to have to endure another day of it.

He found Leon and Nicky and sat down with them, filling them in on his encounters with Sammie and Luke.

"She kissed you, huh?" Nicky said with a mischievous grin and a wiggle of his eyebrows behind his thick glasses.

"Yeah. It was kind of . . . weird," Kevin said.

"What's weird about being kissed by a girl? I think about it all the time," Leon said.

Kevin shrugged.

"I guess I never have," he said. "Besides, Sammie's my friend."

"She's a girl," Nicky reminded him.

"And she's your date for prom," Leon added.

"I keep telling you, it's not a date. We're just both going. Together."

"I don't think Sammie knows that," Nicky said.

"Sure she does. I mean, I'm also going with you guys, but you're not my dates, right?"

"No, but then, first of all, we're guys, and second, we have dates," Leon said slowly.

"I'm just saying, me, you, and Sammie do everything together. We hang out, go to the movies, whatever," Kevin said in exasperation. "So what makes the prom any different?"

Leon looked at Nicky and shook his head.

"It's like trying to explain algebra to a chimpanzee." He sighed.

"Listen, dude, just because Sammie knows all the characters on *Star Voyagers* and reads comic books doesn't make her one of the guys, okay?" Nicky said.

"In case you missed health class the day they explained it, boys and girls are different," Leon agreed. "They take stuff like dances and dating real serious."

"Since when did you guys become experts

on girls?" Kevin said with a laugh.

"We're not," Leon said. "But we do know the difference between hanging out and a date, and a guy asking a girl to prom is a date."

"Yo! Keller!"

Kevin winced at the sound of the voice that cut through the din of the crowded lunchroom. Leon and Nicky turned to look at its source, but Kevin didn't have to in order to recognize it as belonging to Elliot Kingman.

"See you at the prom!" Elliot shouted, followed by the loud laughter of him and his buddies.

"That's original," Leon muttered.

"Just ignore him," Kevin said.

"It's like trying to ignore a toothache," Nicky grumbled.

The next thing they knew, Elliot and his friends were looming behind them at their table.

"You *are* gonna be there, aren't you, Kevvy?" Elliot demanded.

Kevin kept staring straight ahead, his lips pressed in a thin, hard line.

"You better be, little man, 'cause if you're not, I'll give you twice as much when I get my hands on you on Monday," Elliot said.

Kevin didn't respond, not even when Elliot banged the back of his head with his elbow as he walked away in a flurry of laughter and high fives with his pals.

Nicky looked at him with wide, frightened eyes.

"What was that all about?"

"Nothing," Kevin said.

"That was definitely something," Leon croaked.

"It's no big deal. He said he's going to get his payback at the prom, that's all," Kevin replied. He tried to sound casual, even though his heart was pounding and his throat felt tight.

"What're you gonna do?" Nicky said. "You gotta tell somebody . . ."

"He's not going to do anything," Kevin said. "There's gonna be, like, a hundred teachers and parents chaperoning the dance. Besides, Elliot's just finishing a week of detention for what he did to Luke McPhee and can't afford to get caught picking on someone else again so soon. I figure as long as I stay in the gym, he can't touch me."

"I don't know," Leon said doubtfully.

But Kevin just shrugged and said, "Don't worry about it."

He only wished he felt as confident as he sounded.

# Chapter 12

"Wow, this is probably the first time in my life that I've ever *wanted* to be in a school gym," Leon said.

Standing beside him, Wendy Butler's eyes were wide with wonder.

"This is so cool," she said. "I'm so glad you asked me, Leon!"

The middle school gymnasium had been transformed from its usual brown tile wall and polished wood floor drabness into an exciting and colorfully decorated club atmosphere. Hundreds of crepe-paper banners and balloons splashed bright gobs of color across the walls and over the dance floor, while silver-foil streamers caught the glitter of several small rotating spotlights that weaved random patterns of multihued lights across the room.

Students filled the large space, moving on what was usually center court to the pulsing beat of the dance music being spun by a DJ, or mingling on the sidelines with fruit punch and snacks. Keeping a watchful eye out were the teachers and parents volunteering as chaperones, making sure the celebrating students were on their best behavior so that everyone had a good time.

After presenting their tickets and having their hands stamped, Kevin and Sammie came in right behind Leon and Wendy. Sammie gave a small gasp of delight and reached for his hand, an action that Kevin barely noticed. He was too busy scanning the dimly lighted and packed gymnasium for other familiar faces.

For one familiar face in particular.

Despite the brave front he put on for his friends, Kevin had been sick to his stomach with worry since his encounter yesterday in the lunchroom with Elliot. He could hardly sleep last night and had spent most of the day trying to think of a reason not to be here now. But no matter what excuse he came up with, the whole school would still know the truth: that he had ditched the prom because he was afraid of Elliot Kingman.

The crazy thing was, whether or not he showed up tonight, everyone still knew it. While he'd been taunted to his face on Thursday, yesterday it was the whispering behind his back that had made him miserable. Right after lunch, Elliot and his friends told everyone what was planned for Kevin, and the news had spread like wildfire. Even now, he felt like everybody was watching him, just waiting for Elliot to make good on his threat.

"Are you okay, Kevin?" Sammie whispered.

"Huh? Oh yeah. Sure," Kevin said with a forced smile.

"You know you're not a very good liar, don't you?"

"Really, Sammie, I'm fine," he insisted.

"Then stop looking around like you expect wild tigers to jump on you any second."

"Look, as long as we stay in the gym around the chaperones, Elliot can't touch me, so let's just have fun," Kevin said.

Nicky and Cheryl appeared from out of the crowd on the dance floor and hurried toward them. Despite the fact that his taped-up glasses were askew and his oversize hand-me-down dress shirt was hanging out of the waistband of his too-large chinos, Nicky couldn't have looked happier. He and Cheryl were both out of breath and smiling broadly.

"Where have you guys been?" he shouted over the music. "You're missing all the fun."

"Have you been . . . dancing?" Leon gasped in disbelief.

"Yeah, Cheryl showed me how. It's easy! C'mon, we'll teach you," Nicky said.

Leon looked around uncomfortably, his face brightening as soon as he caught sight of the refreshment table loaded with a variety of homemade cookies, brownies, and cupcakes.

"Uh, maybe later, dude," he said and, with a giggling Wendy in tow, made a beeline for the snacks.

"Do you want to dance, Kevin?" Sammie asked.

Kevin grinned in embarrassment.

"I don't think so, I mean, I . . . uh, don't really know how," he said.

Sammie took his hand and started to pull him toward the dance floor. "If Nicky can do it, so can you."

"That's for sure! And everyone knows I'm king of the spazzes. Come on, Cheryl," Nicky said, and he and his date jumped back into the crowd.

"Please, do we have to? I don't think I can . . . I'll just feel like such a dork out there with everybody watching me," Kevin said, resisting impatient Sammie's tugs.

"Nobody's going to be watching you," Sammie said. "They're all too busy having fun to care what you look like."

"Come on, Sammie . . ."

Sammie put her hands on her hips and gave him a hard look.

"What's the point of coming to a dance if we don't dance?" she demanded.

"I told you! I'll feel dorky doing . . . that," he said, looking miserably at the nearest dancers, gyrating to the pounding music.

"Do *they* look dorky to you?"

"Honestly? Yeah."

"So if everybody's dorky, who's going to care if you are, too? Now, let's go," she ordered.

With a groan of surrender, Kevin let Sammie pull him onto the floor, where she started to dance.

"Just do what I'm doing," she instructed. "Just feel the music and move with it. Start with your feet."

"Okay," he said skeptically, looking down at

her feet and at those of the kids around him. Slowly at first, he started to shuffle them and, pretty soon, had them moving more or less in time to the beat of the music.

Sammie flashed him a big smile of approval.

"Okay, now try loosening your legs and letting your hips move, too."

It took a couple of songs for him to get the hang of that, but by then he was so focused on what he was doing, he had forgotten all about feeling self-conscious. Before long and without even being told, his arms and shoulders were also moving in time to the music.

"Hey," he cried out in surprise. "I'm dancing!"

Sammie laughed and gave him a thumbs-up. *Maybe*, he thought with a grin, *this isn't going to be so bad after all.*

● ● ●

Several songs later, it was Sammie who wanted to take a break from dancing.

"Still think dancing is dorky?" Sammie asked as they went to join Leon and Wendy on the sidelines.

"Uh-uh," he said. "It's actually pretty cool. You should try it, Leon."

Leon licked some cupcake frosting from his fingers and shook his head.

"No thanks. I still haven't checked out the brownies."

"Do you need us to help you drag him out there, Wendy?" Sammie asked Leon's date.

"That's okay, we're having fun right here." Wendy smiled.

As Leon and Kevin poured cups of punch for themselves and the girls, Leon said, "I didn't believe Sammie when she said she was gonna wear a dress. She looks real nice tonight."

"Oh yeah. I guess she does," Kevin said, glancing in her direction. "Hey, have you seen Timmy around? I wanted to say hello to him."

"Do you really think you should, after what Gail did to you the other day?"

"That wasn't his fault," Kevin said, looking carefully around the gym, trying to locate the other boy.

"Maybe not, but he's gonna be with her, you know."

He finally spotted Timmy on the other side of the room, talking with a group of his teammates and their dates. Gail Rollins was at his side, hanging on to his arm like she owned him.

"I don't care," Kevin said. "The whole reason I wanted to come to this thing was to hang out with him. You coming with me?"

Leon made a face and said, "No thanks."

"What's your problem with Timmy all of a sudden?"

"Nothing," Leon said. "I just want to stay here, that's all."

"Fine," Kevin snapped. "I'm going."

● ● ●

Gail Rollins turned and saw Kevin walking toward their group. Smirking, she leaned over and said something to the girl next to her. That girl looked at Kevin and laughed, and then all the kids with Timmy were looking his way.

Timmy barely glanced at him before taking Gail's hand and leading her quickly onto the dance floor.

Kevin froze in surprise.

What was *that* about?

The other boy had seen him, he was sure of that. So why would he suddenly decide he had to dance now, when he knew Kevin was on his way over to see him?

Unless . . .

Kevin swallowed hard. His throat felt tight and his eyes burned.

Sammie was right. Timmy Baker didn't want any of the kids he hung out with to know they were friends!

# Chapter 13

"Kevin! What's wrong?"

Kevin couldn't bring himself to even look at Sammie as he hurried past her, pushing through the crush of kids around the dance floor. All he wanted was to get out of there and as far away from her and his humiliation as possible. The last thing in the world he could do right now was admit to Sammie that Timmy had so cruelly and obviously ditched him.

Kevin raced from the gymnasium and down the hallway. He just needed to be left alone and to get some fresh air.

And he needed to figure out how he could have been so clueless about Timmy!

Sure, the handsome and popular boy had always been nice to him, but why hadn't he seen that it was always on Timmy's terms? It was obvious now that he was embarrassed of the Geek Squad when anyone else was around, and hung out with them only when he wanted to borrow some comics from Kevin's collection. And Kevin was always the one inviting Timmy to come with them to the comic shop. He tried really hard to be Timmy's friend, but the other boy never made any effort in return.

And what about last Wednesday? Sammie was right . . . Timmy *had* lied to him about having a practice to get out of going to Comics Universe with them and then lied to him again when they ran into each other at the mall. And if Timmy had been unaware of Kevin's daylong humiliation by the taunts of "see you at the prom," then he would have been the only one in their grade who was.

"Stupid, stupid, stupid," Kevin muttered miserably to himself, stalking out the front doors and into the cool night air.

The thing is, he really liked Timmy. He was the kind of kid Kevin always *wanted* to be like and to be liked by . . . but he should have known better. His other friends did. Leon and Nicky never chased after Timmy's friendship, and Sammie had even tried warning him about the swim-team captain.

So why had Kevin been so blind to what everyone else could plainly see?

And why did being snubbed by Timmy hurt as much as it did?

Kevin wasn't paying any attention to where he was walking. He needed time to think and his only destination was getting as far away from everybody else as possible.

"What's the matter, punk, gonna cry?"

Kevin had just turned the corner on the walkway that went around the side of the school building when he heard those words. At first, lost in his thoughts, Kevin thought they were being addressed to him, but when he looked up he saw he wasn't their intended target.

Up ahead, just outside the pool of light cast by a lamppost, was a group of boys, huddled in a circle. Kevin couldn't see their faces in the dim light, but he knew that voice.

Somehow, in the excitement of the moment, he had momentarily forgotten the threat of Elliot Kingman hanging over his head. He had no doubt Elliot remembered, but it looked as though Kevin wasn't the only person on the bully's list tonight. He couldn't see who they had surrounded now, trapped and forced to listen to their taunts and jeering laughter, but he was sure he would be next if any of them spotted him.

"You think you're too good to talk to me," he heard Elliot snarl. "Well, this time I'm gonna make you talk. You'll be *begging* me to leave you alone!"

Kevin stepped back into the deeper shadows against the wall just as the crowd of boys parted and a smaller figure stumbled backward out of the group and fell to one knee on the pavement.

"C'mon, McWeenie, I'm waiting!" Elliot demanded, stepping forward and looming over Luke McPhee.

Kevin held his breath. He couldn't believe this was happening again . . . but this time, it was unlikely that any teachers would happen by to stop what was about to happen.

"Last chance, McWeenie!" Elliot said, his fists clenched at his sides. The other boys urged him on with their laughter and comments.

But Luke remained silent, either too scared or too proud to obey.

"Okay, you had your chance, you little pansy," Elliot growled, and took a step toward him.

Kevin wasn't exactly sure what happened next, but with an enraged cry and swinging fists, Luke suddenly hurled himself at Elliot.

Luke's first blows landed on the bigger boy's chest and shoulders but seemed to surprise Elliot more than hurt him. It wasn't until one of his punches grazed Elliot's cheek that he snapped out of his amazement and reacted.

With a grunt, he shoved the wildly swinging Luke away from him and, flashing a nasty smile of satisfaction, threw several punches of his own. The first one slammed into Luke's shoulder, throwing him off balance, while the next landed on his chest with a dull thud that Kevin could hear a dozen yards away. Luke staggered back, gasping, until the next blow smashed into his nose and sent him crumbling to the ground on his hands and knees.

Kevin felt paralyzed and once again ashamed of his cowardice. He wanted to help . . . but he was scared of sharing in the beating that Luke was taking.

But because Luke had thrown the first punches, it seemed as if Elliot felt he could just keep hitting the weaker boy. He pulled back his fist as he grabbed a handful of Luke's shirt to haul him to his feet.

*If only there was a teacher or another adult around*, Kevin thought miserably.

Or even if they *thought* one was near . . . !

"Look out!" Kevin shouted from the shadows. "Principal's coming!"

Elliot let go of Luke's shirt, and with panicked looks all around, he and his friends ran off. Kevin breathed a sigh of relief that they had taken off toward the back of the school, away from where he was hidden.

As soon as they were out of sight, Kevin ran over to Luke. He has still on his hands and knees, his head hanging down and his shoulders heaving with silent sobs.

"Luke! Hey, you okay?" Kevin said, kneeling next to him.

Luke looked at him, tears running down his face and a trickle of blood dripping from his nose.

"Leave me alone," he sobbed.

"Come on," Kevin said, trying to help the crying boy to his feet. "Let's go inside before they—"

But Luke pulled free, shouting, "I said leave me alone! I shouldn't have come . . . but you said . . . forget it!"

"I . . . I'm sorry, Luke. If you would've told me you were coming tonight, my dad could have picked you up."

Luke swiped his sleeve across his bleeding nose and shook his head.

"It . . . it's not your fault. It's mine . . . 'cause of what I am . . . ," Luke whimpered.

"You didn't do anything. Elliot's been picking on you ever since I can remember," Kevin said. "Please, let's go inside. You can clean up, and then we'll . . ."

"Elliot's right!" Luke shouted, lurching to his feet.

"Right about what?" Kevin asked, confused.

"About what I am!" Luke sobbed bitterly.

"Stop it, Luke. Elliot's a total jerk. Don't listen to anything he says."

Luke whirled on Kevin, his face twisted in misery and pain, and screamed, "I *am* a pansy! I'm gay, okay?"

Kevin reeled back, stunned, and before he could respond, Luke ran away into the night.

# Chapter 14

He found Sammie where he had left her, with Leon and Wendy near the refreshment table.

"Where did you go?" Sammie demanded. "We tried to find you, but you were gone."

"I can't stay here. I . . . I've got to go home," Kevin said.

"What happened, dude?" Leon asked. "Oh man, don't tell me Elliot . . . ?"

"You guys stay. I . . . I just don't feel so good, that's all," Kevin said.

"That's okay," Sammie said softly. "I'll go with you."

"Yeah, sure, we can go someplace else," Leon said, Wendy at his side nodding in agreement.

But Kevin shook his head, unable to look his friends in the eye.

"No, I want to be alone, okay?" he muttered, and turned to hurry away from them.

He only made it as far as the front door. "I been looking for you, Keller," Elliot snarled.

As Kevin tried to leave the school, the bigger boy blocked the walkway outside the main entrance, his buddies spread out around him. Kevin was pretty sure he couldn't have outrun any of them even if there was anyplace to go.

He started to take a step back into the safety of the school and the chaperones . . .

But then what?

"Let's go, fatso! I owe you big-time for all the trouble you got me into!" Elliot snapped. The insult about his weight was almost as painful as any blow the bigger boy might land.

He couldn't keep running forever. And even if he was able to avoid Elliot for as long as he lived in Medford, so what? Wherever the family moved to next, there would just be another bully waiting for him there. And at all the places after that.

That had been true up to now, and it wasn't going to change.

Unless . . . it was Kevin who changed. Wasn't

that what his father had been trying to tell him last week?

*No matter how fast you might be, you're never fast enough to outrun your troubles. It's better to be the kind of man who does the right thing and faces his problems head on,* Colonel Keller had said.

So face them, Kevin told himself now. Get it over with! He had seen what Elliot had done to Luke with his words and fists. The same thing he thought he could do to anyone because they were afraid to stand up to him.

That's what Mr. Gallagher had told his English class during the discussion of *To Kill a Mockingbird.*

*All that is necessary for evil to triumph is for good men to do nothing,* the teacher had quoted.

It was about time Kevin did something!

"You got into trouble for picking on Luke," Kevin said, amazed at how calm and steady his voice sounded.

Elliot took a step toward him, his face twisted in anger.

"I got in trouble because *you* ratted me out to Mr. Teitelbaum," he said.

"No, I didn't, but I am telling what you did to Luke tonight."

That stopped Elliot dead in his tracks, but only for a second.

"You tell and you'll be sorry," he threatened.

"You're already gonna beat me up. How much *more* sorry can you make me?" Kevin said with a harsh laugh.

All around him, his friends snorted and groaned.

"Total *diss*, Kingman!" one said.

"You gonna *take* that, dude?" another shouted.

"He burned you, man!" added a third.

Elliot's already angry expression darkened and his face flushed bright red. He growled, "You're a dead man, Keller!"

He ran at Kevin, raising his fist. Kevin took one step to the side and, hoping he remembered what else his father had been teaching him all week on the lawn of their backyard, grabbed hold of Elliot's forearm. He stepped back in toward the attacking boy and leaned his hip into his body, using Elliot's own forward motion and speed to send him flipping through the air with a startled yelp.

Elliot hit the ground on his rear end, his breath exploding from his lungs with a loud "Uhff!"

There was a momentary stunned silence. Elliot's crew looked first at their downed leader and then back at Kevin in disbelief. Elliot just shook his head. He was dazed and unable to figure out how he had gotten down there on the pavement.

But Elliot's confusion only lasted until the first of his friends started laughing again.

"Dude! Did Keller just kick your butt?" one of them hooted.

"He . . . he tripped me," Elliot said defensively as he started to climb back to his feet.

"Naw, man, he kung-fued you!" another one said, laughing.

Elliot's eyes were burning with humiliation and rage as he turned them on Kevin. "This little pansy can't kung-fu squat," he rumbled, using that hateful word for the second time that night. Hearing it aimed at him infuriated Kevin as much as being called fatso had.

This time when Elliot charged Kevin, he kept his arms close to his sides so the smaller boy wouldn't be able to throw him again.

So Kevin tripped him instead, leaning back out of harm's way while sticking his foot between Elliot's ankles, just as his father had showed him.

Elliot yelled and stumbled past him, his arms windmilling wildly to keep his balance.

Kevin turned to keep Elliot in sight, his heart pounding. He didn't know how long he could keep this up, and if Elliot's pals decided to help him, he was definitely toast. But he had gone too far to back down now, and even if he did wind up taking a beating, at least he wouldn't go down without having fought back.

But just as he feared, Elliot's buddies were starting to close in around the fighting boys. They may have thought it was funny, but they weren't about to let Kevin get away with winning for very long. All of their reputations would be ruined if someone like Kevin Keller could whip any one of them.

"Leave him alone!"

Word of the fight must have spread to the dance inside because kids were hurrying out to see what was going on. Leading the crowd were Sammie, Leon, and Nicky, and it was Sammie who had spoken up.

"Yeah . . . what *she* said," Nicky shouted.

"Uh, yeah! Me three," Leon added.

"Shut up, geeks, or we'll pound you, too!" Elliot ordered.

Sammie took a step toward him.

"Go ahead, Elliot—pound me! I dare you!" she said defiantly.

For a second, Kevin was afraid Elliot was going to take her up on her dare, but just then, Timmy Baker pushed his way to the front of the crowd and stepped between Elliot and the Geek Squad.

"Stop it, Elliot!" he said. "Leave them alone."

"Butt out, Timmy. This is none of your business," Elliot snapped.

"Yeah, it is," Timmy said, with an apologetic look at Kevin. "These guys are my friends."

"These freaks? You're kidding!" Elliot said with a nasty laugh.

"Stop picking on these kids or you'll find out. Just go away, man."

"Who died and made you boss?" one of Elliot's friends shouted.

"I'm not the boss . . . and neither are you guys," Timmy said. "And if anybody's a freak, it's a bully who picks on smaller kids just because they're different."

The rest of the crowd closed around Timmy, Kevin, and the others. All of a sudden, the Geek Squad was surrounded by kids cheering them on and booing and shouting down Elliot and his crew.

It felt like a dream to Kevin. Heck, it *had* to be . . . where else but in a dream could Kevin Keller be the hero while the big, bad bullies were chased off by his cheering friends and admirers?

# Chapter 15

By the time any of the chaperones got outside, the crowd had already started to break up and head back in to the dance.

"I . . . I'm really sorry for the way I acted," Timmy said to Kevin and his friends as they walked back to the gym.

"Are you kidding?" Leon exclaimed. "You just saved Kevin from getting totaled out there."

Timmy grinned at Kevin and slapped him on the shoulder. Kevin blushed at the touch of the other boy's hand.

"Kevin saved himself," he said proudly. "I'm just sorry I wasn't a better friend before that. I mean, I know I didn't treat you guys right . . ."

"No, you didn't," Sammie agreed.

"Hey, that's okay, you were there when it counted," Kevin said quickly, jumping to his defense.

"But I wasn't. I knew how Elliot was treating you and some of the other kids, but I never really said anything about it. I mean, yeah, if I saw him picking on someone, I might tell him to leave them alone, but I should have done more," Timmy said.

"So why didn't you?" Sammie said angrily.

"Because . . . I was afraid," Timmy said softly.

"You? Of what?" Leon exclaimed in disbelief.

"Yeah, like anybody was gonna pick on you!" Nicky scoffed.

"It's gonna sound stupid." Timmy looked away in embarrassment.

Just minutes earlier Kevin had realized that Timmy hadn't treated the Geek Squad the way a real friend should . . . and now he suddenly realized why.

"Because," Kevin said, "you were afraid if you were nice to us, the kids you hang out with would stop being friends with you!"

Timmy nodded. "Yeah. Stupid, right?"

"Holy crud," Nicky said, his eyes wide behind the thick lenses of his glasses. "You mean even cool kids and jocks have to worry about stuff like that? Man, what hope do we have?"

As they were about to go back into the dance, Gail Rollins was leaving. She looked at Timmy and then at his companions.

"You know it's really rude to ditch the people you came with," she said to him coldly. "I don't know if I want to forgive you . . . especially if you left me standing in the middle of the dance floor for *them*."

Gail waved her hand in the direction of Kevin and the others, as if pointing to an unpleasant mess someone had left on her lawn.

"Yeah, sorry about that, but I had to apologize," Timmy replied.

"What for?" she asked in surprise.

"For everything. And I think you also owe Kevin an apology," he said.

"Like, I don't think so!" Gail scoffed.

Timmy shrugged and turned back to the Geek Squad.

"Come on, guys, let's go. Hey, Kevin, would you mind if I danced with Sammie?" Timmy asked.

"Um . . . it's okay with me if it's okay with her," Kevin replied.

Sammie smiled and, with a satisfied look at the stunned and suddenly speechless Gail, said, "Thanks, Timmy, I'd love to!"

And the Geek Squad, with its newest

member in tow, went back into the dance.

● ● ●

As Colonel Keller's car turned onto Maple Lane, Kevin, in the passenger seat, pointed at the house ahead of them.

"That's where Luke lives, Dad," he said.

His father nodded and pulled up in front of the weathered green house, his car's headlights sweeping over the ramshackle fence and overgrown lawn. It looked even worse in the dark of night than it had during the day.

"Oh!" In the backseat, Sammie gave a quiet, involuntary gasp of surprise at the sight that greeted them.

Kevin had gone looking for Luke while Sammie and Timmy danced, first checking the restrooms where the bloodied boy might have gone to clean up, then looking around the grounds. When he couldn't find him, Kevin used the pay phone in the school lobby to call home and asked his father to pick him up and help in the search. While he waited for his dad to get there, Kevin went back inside to tell his friends where he was going. Sammie immediately volunteered to go with him, but it was Timmy's proud smile of approval that gave Kevin the most satisfaction.

"I don't even know if he's going to want to talk to me," Kevin said, opening the door.

"Do you want me to come with you?" Sammie asked.

"Thanks, Sammie, but I think I better talk to him alone," he said. He hadn't told anyone else the secret Luke had screamed out to him before running off. It wasn't his reveal, and he was afraid if he showed up at the door with another person, Luke would send them both away.

"Take as much time as you need, Kev," his father said.

Kevin nodded and stepped out onto the sidewalk.

He made his way carefully up the cracked walk in the dim light of the single, bare bulb over the front door. There were a few lights visible through the windows, and he could hear the sound of a television blaring from inside.

Where there once had been a doorbell Kevin found only a hole in the doorframe and a couple of dangling wires, so he knocked. The TV went silent, so he knocked again, and a few moments later the door opened.

It was answered by a girl, about ten years old, who shared Luke's brown hair and large, sad eyes. She had to be the sister Luke had mentioned.

"What do you want?" she asked.

"Hi. I'm a friend of Luke's. Is he home?"

She shook her head.

"Do you know where he is?"

She shook her head again.

"Are your parents home?"

"Daddy is, but he's watching TV."

From inside the house, a man shouted in an angry voice, "Who is it?"

"A boy looking for Luke," the girl shouted back.

"Tell him he's not here and close the door!" the man shouted.

The girl looked at him, shrugged, and slammed the door in his face.

With a worried frown, Kevin hurried back to the car.

● ● ●

"Do you have any idea where else Luke might be?" Colonel Keller asked as they drove away from the house on Maple Lane.

"I don't really know him that well. I mean, we've only talked a few times, usually at school," Kevin said.

"Wait . . . didn't you say you saw him at Waverly Park the other day when you went there to look for me?" Sammie said.

"Oh, right. But it closes at sundown," he said.

"Right, like we've never hopped the fence after closing."

Kevin nodded.

"Dad? Would you mind . . . ?"

"Just tell me where to go, kiddo," Colonel Keller said.

●●●

With the flashlight from the emergency kit the colonel kept in his trunk, they approached the locked gate of the park. By day, the place was filled with happily barking, playful dogs, but after dark it was deserted and still. The park was surrounded by a four-foot-high stone wall that was there to keep the dogs inside, but nothing could prevent after-hours visitors from climbing over it.

Kevin was glad he had called his father. The park, with only a few streetlights to illuminate the perimeter, was filled with shadows that seemed to move with the swaying of the trees in the night breeze. He would have hated to be there by himself or with just Sammie for company. His mind told him he wasn't in any danger, but the thumping of his heart was louder than any logic.

Colonel Keller led the way, sweeping the beam of his flashlight back and forth over the open lawn and poking it into the shadows around trees and shrubs.

"Look!" Sammie said, grabbing Kevin's arm and pointing to one of the benches at the far end of the park.

At first Kevin couldn't tell if it was just another shadow from the surrounding trees or if someone was there. His father quickly turned the flashlight on the huddled shape.

It was Luke!

Kevin's first thought was to be relieved, but then he realized that the boy was slumped on the bench in an awkward, unnatural position and didn't react when the light swept over him.

His father realized something was wrong as well.

"Stay here!" he ordered as he sprinted

across the grass toward the prone boy.

Colonel Keller knelt next to the boy, patting his cheek with his fingertips and gently speaking his name. When that got no response, he reached for Luke's wrist to check his pulse. Kevin and Sammie heard his gasp of surprise and watched as he reached into his pocket and pulled out his cell phone.

"Hello, nine-one-one?" he said urgently. "I need an ambulance at Waverly Park . . ."

# Chapter 16

Kevin had only been in an emergency room once before in his life. It was when he was eight years old and had broken his arm in a fall from a swing set in the backyard of a friend's house. That time, on a sunny summer weekday afternoon, a nurse had taken him and his mother straight back to an examination room, closing a curtain around them that blocked out the sight of the other patients. He remembered being examined by a lady doctor with kind green eyes, having his arm x-rayed and then wrapped in a cast that he wore like a trophy through the rest of the summer and into the start of the school year. And every step of the way, someone would hand him a lollipop as a reward for being brave and letting the doctors do their jobs.

But this Saturday night, there were no lollipops or kind-eyed doctors as Kevin and Sammie sat side by side in the hard plastic chairs in the waiting room of Medford General Hospital's E.R. Instead, there was a selection of pained and dazed-looking people holding bloodied rags or ice packs to wounds and aches, a shivering man with a ragged cough that wouldn't stop, and a mother cradling a crying little boy. The nurses and aides were all getting to these patients as fast as they could, but that could never be fast enough for those not feeling well.

"I can't believe Luke would hurt himself like that," Sammie said softly.

"Me neither. I knew he was sad about . . . about stuff, but I never thought it was this bad," Kevin agreed.

"Did he tell you what was wrong?"

Kevin shrugged, then nodded.

"Yeah. After Elliot beat him up, he told me. But . . . don't ask me what it was, okay? I mean, I know we're friends and shouldn't have any secrets, but what he said was . . . real private, you know?"

"I think so. Anyway, it's okay for friends to have some secrets. I . . . I've kind of kept one from you."

"Yeah?"

"Yeah. I . . . I like you, Kevin. A lot."

"I like you, too, Sammie. That's why we're friends." Kevin smiled.

"Except, I like you . . . like this."

And the next thing he knew, Sammie was kissing him, her lips pressed against his. The kiss lasted only a few seconds, and then Sammie pulled away, looking at him with a mixture of expectation and embarrassment.

"Well? Aren't you going to say something?" she asked anxiously.

But Kevin didn't know what to say. Kissing him was the last thing he expected her to do and, he realized with a start, not something he had ever thought about. Leon and Nicky talked about the girls they liked and he wondered sometimes why he didn't share their fascination with the subject. He had always just assumed that everybody was different and, sooner or later, his interest in girls would awaken.

"Kevin . . . ?"

Sammie was exactly the kind of person he *should* be interested in as a girlfriend. He could talk to her endlessly about anything. She was funny, smart, talented, cute . . . they shared all the same interests.

So what was wrong with Sammie that he just couldn't manage to summon those kinds of feelings for her?

Even when it came to taking her to the prom, he had only asked Sammie so he would have an excuse to hang out with Timmy, whose approval and attention he was always trying to get. As usual, just the thought of the other boy made him smile and feel . . .

"Oh. Wow!" he suddenly exclaimed.

"What's wrong?" Sammie asked.

It was like someone had flipped a switch in his brain.

Timmy. *Not* Sammie!

And with that, he felt as though a great weight had been lifted from his shoulders, and for the first time in his confused life, he actually understood who he really was.

"Kevin?" Sammie said, staring at him.

"Sammie . . . we have to talk . . . !"

● ● ●

Clutching the oversize envelope in his hands, Kevin stuck his head into the hospital room. Luke was lying in a bed under bright white sheets, wearing a crisp blue hospital gown, and his wrists were bandaged with clean dressings. His face was turned toward the window. Kevin couldn't tell if he was asleep. Next to the bed, a beeping monitor on a stand was attached to the thin, pale boy by wires that disappeared under his gown. A second stand held a bag of clear fluid that dripped into a plastic tube taped to his arm.

It had been well after midnight before Colonel Keller finally rejoined Kevin and Sammie in the waiting room. Luke's father had been called, but instead of showing any concern for his son, he had just started screaming and cruelly berating him for what he had tried to do. The social worker assigned to Luke by the hospital had to have the irate Mr. McPhee removed from the treatment room. Kevin's father had stayed by the boy's bedside while the doctors took care of his wounds.

Luke hadn't cut himself very deeply, but badly enough that he wouldn't have survived the night alone on that bench if they hadn't found him when they did.

"Hey, you awake?" Kevin asked softly.

Luke turned and looked at Kevin.

"Hi. Is it okay if I come in?"

"Sure. I mean, you did save my life," Luke said with a shrug.

"That would've mostly been my dad, but I'm glad we found you."

"I'm not so sure I am."

"Don't talk like that, Luke. I don't have that many friends that I want to lose even one," Kevin said. "Especially that way."

Luke's eyes were filling with tears that he didn't bother to wipe away.

"Why would you want to be my friend . . . especially after I told you about . . . about what I am?" he asked.

"Luke, it doesn't matter that you're gay."

"Yes, it does. Everybody'll hate me. You heard what Elliot called me!"

"I told you, he's a total jerk and stuff like being gay or straight only matters to total jerks. Everybody else is going to like you for who you are, not who you love. Anyway, Elliot's not going to be bothering you anymore. I told the social worker what he did to you at the dance last night and we're going to be reporting it to the school tomorrow."

Luke's eyes went wide.

"You . . . you did that for me?"

"Sure," Kevin said with a smile. "That's what friends do. Besides, you didn't hear what happened after you ran off."

Luke shook his head and used the edge of his sheet to wipe his eyes as Kevin told him the story of his own encounter with Elliot and his friends in front of the school. The thin boy started to smile as Kevin described how he had used the judo his father taught him to knock the bigger boy to the ground. By the time he finished up with Timmy and Sammie's dance, Luke was laughing.

"You're kidding? *Timmy Baker* danced with Sammie Warren . . . in front of the whole class?"

"Yeah. You should've seen Gail and the cheerleaders, dude. I thought their heads were gonna explode." Kevin laughed. "Oh, and speaking of Sammie, she made this for you."

He handed Luke the large envelope he had been carrying. Surprised, Luke took it and opened it, gasping with shock and delight at the sight of the card. It read "Get Well and Get Back to School" in giant red letters over a drawing of Luke being carried on the shoulders of the Geek Squad, surrounded by a crowd of cheering students.

"Open it. Everybody signed it," Kevin said.

"Well, you know, everybody we could get it to before I came to visit."

Luke looked at the dozens of signatures and well wishes that were written inside and his eyes started to fill with tears again.

"I . . . I don't believe it," he said in a voice shaking with emotion. "You didn't tell anybody . . . what I said, did you?"

"No, but only because I figure that's up to you to tell who you want to know, not because I think it's anything to be ashamed of."

"Thanks," Luke said.

"Actually, I've got to thank you. I mean, it took a lot of guts for you to tell me you're gay, and that kind of gave me the courage to finally start thinking about some things about myself."

"Like what?"

"I'm not really completely sure yet, but as soon as I figure it out, I"ll let you know."

Luke looked down at the homemade greeting card in his lap.

"It's been forever since I had any friends. I just hope I remember how it's done," he said softly.

"I may not be sure of a lot of things yet, but I do know this much, Luke . . . the easiest way to *have* friends is just to be one."

# Epilogue

"Yes?" Veronica Lodge asked eagerly. "*Then* what happened?"

"We all lived happily ever after!" Kevin exclaimed with a laugh.

"Don't give us any of that fairy-tale junk," Jughead said as he finished packing the last of the unused decorations into a plastic storage bin. "What happened to everybody?"

"Well, I moved around a few more times before we settled here in Riverdale and . . ." Kevin teased.

"You know what we mean, wise guy!" Veronica said. "Did you and Luke stay friends? What did Sammie say when she found out you were gay? Did you ever tell Timmy how you felt about him? What happened to Elliot? *Finish* the story, buster!"

"Okay, okay. Luke came back to school a few days later and with the help of some therapy and patience, he started to open up and make friends. It also helped a lot that he got away from his abusive father and went to stay with an aunt and uncle who lived in Medford. These days, he's doing well in school and he's even got a boyfriend now."

"So you stayed in touch with him even after you moved away?" Veronica asked.

"Uh-huh. My dad was transferred after the end of that school year, but Luke and I are still in touch on Facebook and in e-mails." Kevin smiled. "It really helped both of us to have a friend who understood what the other was going through. If it hadn't been for him, it would've taken me a lot longer to come to terms with being gay."

"And Timmy . . . ?" Veronica asked coyly.

"Just friends." Kevin sighed. "I eventually came out to him and all the rest of my friends, but Timmy's straight, and I realized that my admitting I had a crush on him would probably have just freaked him out."

"I'll bet Sammie was pretty freaked out by it, too," Jughead said.

"As a matter of fact, Sammie was the first one I told, that night in the hospital, and she not only didn't freak, she totally understood. I think she was kind of relieved to find out that the reason I treated her like a pal and not a girlfriend wasn't because I thought there was something wrong with her but because I just wasn't interested in girls. She started dating someone else a couple of weeks later, but the Geek Squad still all hung out together."

"Which just leaves us with the fate of the evil Elliot Kingman," Veronica said.

"No clue. His parents pulled him out of Medford and sent him to private school. I never saw Elliot again," Kevin said with a shrug.

"So, to quickly sum up, what started out as the world's worst prom night actually ended up with a lot of good coming out of it," Jughead said.

"I guess you could say that," Kevin replied. "Still, there was enough excitement around that prom to last me a lifetime. Now, for *this* one, I've got my eye on a guy to ask who I'm pretty sure won't be freaked out by the invitation."

"I should think so," Veronica said with a smile. "After all, you're a great catch for any guy, Kevin."

"Yep, and the decorations are done!" Jughead announced proudly.

"The place looks amazing," Kevin agreed. "Thanks again, you guys!"

"No need to thank me, Kevin," Jughead said.

"Really?"

"Really . . . but you still need to buy me that cheeseburger you promised!" Jughead grinned. "Let's go. I'm starved."